MICHAEL J. FOX
CHRISTOPHER LLOYD

STEVEN SPIELBERG PRESENTS

A ROBERT ZEMECKIS FILM

MICHAEL J. FOX   CHRISTOPHER LLOYD
"BACK TO THE FUTURE PART III"   MARY STEENBURGEN
THOMAS F. WILSON AND LEA THOMPSON   MUSIC BY ALAN SILVESTRI
EDITED BY ARTHUR SCHMIDT   HARRY KERAMIDAS   PRODUCTION DESIGN BY RICK CARTER
DIRECTOR OF PHOTOGRAPHY DEAN CUNDEY, A.S.C.   EXECUTIVE PRODUCERS STEVEN SPIELBERG
FRANK MARSHALL   KATHLEEN KENNEDY
STORY BY ROBERT ZEMECKIS & BOB GALE
SCREENPLAY BY BOB GALE   PRODUCED BY BOB GALE AND NEIL CANTON
DIRECTED BY ROBERT ZEMECKIS   A UNIVERSAL PICTURE
© 1990 UNIVERSAL CITY STUDIOS INC

AMBLIN ENTERTAINMENT   DOLBY STEREO IN SELECTED THEATRES   Special Visual Effects By INDUSTRIAL LIGHT & MAGIC

A NOVEL BY
CRAIG SHAW GARDNER
BASED ON A SCREENPLAY BY
BOB GALE
STORY BY
ROBERT ZEMECKIS & BOB GALE

B

BERKLEY BOOKS, NEW YORK

BACK TO THE FUTURE PART III

A Berkley Book / published by arrangement with
MCA Publishing Rights, a Division of MCA, Inc.

PRINTING HISTORY
Berkley edition / June 1990

ISBN: 0-425-12240-9

A BERKLEY BOOK® TM 757,375
Berkley Books are published by The Berkley Publishing Group,
200 Madison Avenue, New York, New York 10016.
The name "BERKLEY" and the "B" logo
are trademarks belonging to Berkley Publishing Corporation.

PRINTED IN THE UNITED STATES OF AMERICA

10 9 8 7 6 5 4 3 2 1

"The West is the best."
—JIM MORRISON

•PROLOGUE•

Saturday, November 12, 1955
10:04 P.M.
(AGAIN)

This was *really* déjà vu.

Marty McFly ran down the street, past the malt shop and the movie theater, headed for the courthouse in the center of Hill Valley.

And it was all happening again, just like it did—when? In his past? In his future? When you traveled through time, life could get really confusing.

The clock tower read 10:04.

The DeLorean, with its special superconducting electrical pole added for the occasion, raced past Marty, headed for the electrical line strung across the street. Doc Brown stood thirty-odd feet in the air, on a tall ladder that leaned against the side of the courthouse clock tower, attempting to connect a cable that would supply the DeLorean with all the power it needed to travel through time—back to the future.

Lightning struck the clock tower!

At the last possible second, after almost falling from his ladder perch, Doc Brown connected the cables.

The hook on the pole above the DeLorean hit the electrical line—and 1.21 jigowatts of electricity flooded into the flux capacitor—

and the DeLorean—with another, slightly younger Marty McFly inside—vanished into the future, straight back to 1985, leaving only twin trails of fire where its wheels had been!

Doc Brown went running down the street between the burning trails, yelling at the top of his lungs.

"Ya—haaaaa!"

Marty wished he could be as happy as Doc was now. If only Marty hadn't taken that book of sports statistics when he was in the future. But he had, and Biff Tannen had gotten hold of it, back here in 1955, and—through using the book to bet on sports and make millions—Biff had changed the whole future of Hill Valley!

Marty and Doc had had to come back to the fifties again, to rescue the book from Biff, and restore the future to the way it had been before. And they had succeeded, only to have things go wrong all over again. The DeLorean had been hit by lightning, sending the car with the 1985 version of Doc inside it back seventy years into the past. And Marty was stuck here in 1955 trying to get back home to 1985 all over again.

Marty guessed this was as good a time as any to go up to Doc Brown—the one from 1955—and explain what had really happened.

Marty stepped out of the shadow of the courthouse. He tapped Doc on the shoulder.

Doc turned around, the smile on his face changing to a look of abject horror.

"YAAAAAAAH!" Doc shrieked.

"Calm down, Doc!" Marty urged. "It's me, Marty!"

Doc shook his head wildly. "No! It can't be you! I just sent you back to the future!"

This wasn't going to be easy. Somehow, Marty had to explain everything to the scientist. And the more he thought about it, with the trips he and an older version of Doc Brown had taken to 2015, 1985, and back to 1955 again, the more explaining he knew had to be done.

"Right!" Marty replied, trying to be as logical as possible. "You *did* send me back to the future. But I'm back—back *from* the future!"

"Great Scott!" Doc replied. He staggered back, clutching his chest. He seemed to be having trouble breathing.

"Doc!" Marty called. What was going on?

Doc's eyes rolled up, and he fainted dead away.

"Doc?" Marty asked, but the scientist was out cold. The shock had been too much for him—running into Marty right after he had triumphantly sent that very same Marty into the future—it had been too much for even a scientist like Doc to deal with.

Doc lay very still where he had fallen in the

street. Far too still. What if it was worse than Marty thought, and he couldn't revive his old friend? Then the scientist could never build the time machine in 1985, and Marty would never end up back in 1955 in the first place.

That would be one of those real paradoxes, wouldn't it—the kind that Doc was always warning might put an end to the cosmos and all life as we know it?

"Doc?" Marty called, bending over his fallen friend. "Doc?"

But Doc didn't answer.

This, Marty realized, could get heavy.

•Chapter One•

Sunday, November 13, 1955
7 A.M.

Great Scott!

Doc Emmett L. Brown had to be dreaming.

He was the greatest inventor of all time. Heck, he had actually invented a time machine, although he had designed the device into a car that wouldn't be built for close to thirty years.

Doc Brown frowned in his dream. That was a paradox, wasn't it?

Never mind paradoxes! The time machine worked! He saw the car from the future speed up to eighty-eight miles per hour, then disappear with a boom, leaving only twin trails of flame where the tires had been.

He had sent Marty McFly thirty years into the future—back where he'd come from!

But Marty McFly wouldn't go away! The teenager was right here, all over again, tapping him on the shoulder. Doc backed away. But the kid was behind him! Doc walked away quickly, turning the corner by the malt shop. There was Marty, grinning back.

Marty, Marty, Marty! Where were they all coming from? There had to be an answer. He was a scientist, after all. It had to do with time, didn't it? Yes, that made sense. It was all a matter of—

"Hey, kids, what time is it?"

Doc's eyes snapped open at the sound of the man's bright, cheerful voice. A couple dozen young, high, but no less cheerful voices shouted back: "It's Howdy Doody Time!"

His eyes focused on the black-and-white image of Buffalo Bob Smith, smiling out from the TV set across the room. Rain fell in sheets outside the window of the den—the aftermath, perhaps, of last night's lightning storm? Doc glanced down at his more immediate surroundings. He was sprawled on the living-room couch. There was an obvious deduction to be made from all this: He must have fallen asleep watching television, safe in his own home, far away from lightning storms and time machines and teenagers who refused to go away.

But then why, even after he was awake, did he keep thinking about Marty McFly?

Doc sat up. He remembered. It wasn't a dream after all.

He really had invented a time machine.

"Great Scott!"

Yes! Doctor Emmett Brown, brilliant but sometimes misunderstood scientist, had actually invented something that worked!

He needed to record all of this while it was still fresh in his mind. He jumped up and walked briskly over to the reel-to-reel tape recorder on the other side of the room. He picked up the microphone as he flipped the "record" switch. A quick check of his watch, and he began to dictate:

"Date: Sunday, November thirteenth, 1955, 7:01 A.M. Last night's time travel experiment was apparently a complete success. Lightning struck the clock tower as predicted at precisely 10:04 P.M., making contact with the hook on the time vehicle, which vanished in a brilliant flash of light, leaving a pair of fire trails behind.

"I therefore assume that Marty and the time vehicle were transported forward through time into the year 1985. After that—"

Doc paused. Why did he have that cold feeling in the pit of his stomach? He definitely remembered the lightning, the car disappearing, all of it—up to a point. Doc rubbed his forehead with a frown.

"After that," he spoke into the tape recorder again, "I can't recall what happened." He hesitated, his frown deepening. "In fact, I don't even remember how I got home."

Still, there had to be some explanation.

"Perhaps," Doc theorized, "the jigowatt discharge, coupled with the temporal displacement field generated by the time vehicle caused a disruption of my own brain waves, creating a condition of momentary amnesia—"

As if to contradict his own theory, that one very disturbing moment—the moment after he successfully sent Marty back to the future—came clearly into his brain. He could see the twin lines of flames, so bright in the darkness, feel the coolness of the night air, and something else. There had been a tap on his shoulder. He had turned and seen the teenager all over again. It made no sense.

But, perhaps that very lack of sense supported his theory!

"Indeed," he continued his recitation, "I now recall that moments after the time vehicle disappeared into the future, I saw a vision of Marty, saying he had—come back from the future—"

That's right. Why would a vision say he'd come back from the future? Doc massaged his forehead.

All this seemed to make his brain hurt.

"Undoubtedly, this was some sort of residual image, created by my imagination from the release of my own inner stress—"

It was like the dream, all over again. Doc had a most illogical thought: What if he was still dreaming? What if the nightmare wasn't over?

Marty heard gunfire. For a second, he thought he was stuck in the wrong 1985—the 1985 where Biff had used the sports book to make a fortune and had turned Hill Valley into his own lawless kingdom.

But when he opened his eyes, all he saw was a dusty street, lined on either side by weathered wooden buildings.

A lone figure walked toward him down the street, a figure Marty knew.

"Doc?" Marty called. "Doc Brown?"

But as he walked closer, Marty saw it wasn't Doc Brown, after all. It was Clint Eastwood, wearing a cowboy hat and a sarapé draped over his shoulder.

Marty was in the wild west.

"The heart, Ramone," Clint was saying. "Don't forget the heart."

Why was Clint saying that? Wasn't that from *A Fistful of Dollars*?

There was the sound of gunfire, close by. Somebody was firing on Clint, right at the heart.

"Aim for the heart, Ramone," Clint was saying, "or you'll never stop me."

Ramone kept on firing, and Clint kept on walking. Marty remembered now. Clint had something hidden under the sarapé!

"Undoubtedly," Clint added, "this was some sort of residual image, created by my imagination from the release of my own inner stress—"

That wasn't Clint's voice, was it? Maybe this was Doc Brown after all!

Marty must be dreaming.

He opened his eyes.

"Or perhaps this entire episode has been a dream," Doc Brown continued in his best lecture tone, "brought on by my recent brain-wave experiments. Could I have possibly been asleep for an entire week?"

Marty sat up, rubbing his eyes.

"Hey, Doc?"

Doc spun around as if he had heard a ghost.

"YAAAAH!"

Marty jumped from the overstuffed chair he had been asleep in, careful not to trip over that pink board, hovering quietly, six inches above the carpet.

"It's okay, Doc!" He raised his hands in a gesture of peace. "Calm down. It's me, Marty."

"No, it can't be you!" Doc shook his head vehemently as he threw down the microphone he had been talking into. "I sent you back to the future!"

Marty was getting that feeling of déjà vu again. "That's right," he explained patiently. "But I came back again. Back *from* the future. Don't you remember last night? You fainted and I brought you home."

But Doc's head kept shaking "no" as he marched from the room.

"This can't be happening!" Doc declared. "It's a dream."

Marty turned and followed him.

"It's a *nightmare*," Doc amended. "You can't be here! It doesn't make sense for you to be here!" He walked into the bathroom. "I refuse to even believe you *are* here!"

Doc slammed the door behind him.

It was Marty's turn to shake his head. Doc

couldn't get rid of him that easily. If only his friend would listen to reason!

"But I *am* here, Doc," Marty said, loud enough to penetrate the bathroom door, "and it *does* make sense."

Doc didn't reply, but Marty knew his old friend was too much of a scientist not to listen. Now, all Marty had to do was come up with a simple way to explain all this.

"You see," Marty spoke slowly and carefully, "I came back to 1955, in the time machine *again*, with you—that is, the other you, the you from 1985, because we had to get this book back from Biff which he wasn't supposed to have, which could have ended up screwing everything up in the future. So, after I got the book back, you—that is, the Doc Brown from 1985—you were in the DeLorean and got struck by lightning, and you accidentally got sent back to 1885."

"1885?" Doc's voice called from the other side of the door.

The bathroom door opened. Doc Brown glared down at him.

"It's a very interesting story, future boy, but there's just one little thing that doesn't make sense: If the me of the future is now in the past, how could you possibly know about it?"

Doc was actually facing him! Marty didn't want to miss this chance. He reached inside his jacket pocket.

"You sent me a letter."

He handed the folded yellow envelope to his friend. Doc stared at the aging paper.

"Great Scott!"

The inventor looked like he was going to pass out all over again.

Great Scott!

This was astounding. Doc Brown had to admit it—even with his advanced scientific brain, it had taken him a moment to grasp an idea of this magnitude.

But the letter was certainly in his handwriting. And if his handwriting actually said what he thought he saw in his first cursory glance, why, the implications were enormous!

At the very least, it was very exciting. And an obvious subject for further research. After a hasty breakfast, Doc and Marty adjourned to the laboratory he kept in his garage—Doc did like to keep his scientific endeavors separate from his home life, after all. It was important to keep a proper balance in these things. Now, however, that he was in the proper surroundings, he felt fully justified in pacing about as he read the letter aloud:

" 'Dear Marty, if my calculations are correct, you will receive this letter immediately after you saw the DeLorean struck by lightning.

" 'First, let me assure you that I am alive and well. I have been living happily these past eight months in the year 1885.

" 'The lightning bolt that hit the DeLorean caused a jigowatt overload that scrambled the time circuits, activated the flux capacitor, and sent me back to 1885. The overload shorted out the time circuits and destroyed the flying circuits. Unfortunately, the car will never fly again.' "

Doc frowned and looked over at Marty.

"The car actually flew?"

Marty nodded from where he sat in the over-stuffed chair, that odd pink board still floating by his side.

"You had a hover conversion done in the early twenty-first century," the teenager added helpfully.

Hover conversion? Twenty-first century? Doc Brown nodded in turn, momentarily over-whelmed by the marvels of science.

"Incredible."

But there was more to be learned. He looked back down at the letter.

" 'I set myself up as a blacksmith,' " Doc continued, " 'as a front while I attempted to repair the damage to the time circuits. Unfortunately, this proved impossible because suitable replacement parts will not be invented until 1947. However, I have gotten quite adept at shoeing horses and fixing wagons.' "

Doc looked up again.

"1885. Amazing. I actually end up as a blacksmith in the old west!"

Marty nodded. "Yeah. Pretty heavy, huh?"

Heavy? In 1885? As far as Doc could determine, he would weigh the same—he stopped himself. He had to remember where this Marty McFly came from. Obviously, "heavy" was an expression from the future! Doc could feel that frightening uncertainty creeping back into his brain. There was too much information here, too many things to consider. But there was no time for that—not for a man of science! He quickly returned to reading the letter.

" 'Therefore, I have buried the DeLorean in the abandoned Delgado mine, adjacent to the old Boot Hill Cemetery as shown on the enclosed map. Hopefully, it should remain undisturbed and preserved until you uncover it in 1955.

" 'Inside, you will find repair instructions. My 1955 counterpart—' " Oh. Doc blinked. "That's me," he remarked softly, impressed that he should be addressed by his future self. Or was it his past self? Doc decided he should get back to the letter. " '—should have no problem repairing it so you can drive it back to the future.

" 'Once you have returned to 1985, destroy the time machine.' "

What, all that work to retrieve his greatest invention, and they were going to turn right around and get rid of it? Doc Brown couldn't believe this. He looked up at Marty.

"Destroy it?"

Marty shrugged. "It's a long story, Doc."

Doc Brown shrugged in turn. His brain probably still wasn't quite ready for that long story. His gaze was drawn again to that pink, floating board. He blinked and returned to the letter one more time.

" 'Do not, I repeat, do *not* attempt to come back here and get me. I am perfectly happy living here in the fresh air and wide-open spaces, and I fear that unnecessary time travel only risks further disruption of the space-time continuum.

" 'And please take care of Einstein for me . . .' "

Doc Brown looked up again.

"Einstein?"

"Your dog," Marty explained. "In 1985."

Well, that certainly made sense. "Einstein" was just the sort of name Doc would give to a dog. In 1955, after all, his dog was named Copernicus. And here! It talked about it in the letter:

" 'As you recall,' " Doc continued to read aloud, " 'I left him in my lab in 1985. I know you will give him a good home. Remember to walk him twice a day, and that he only likes canned dog food.

" 'These are my wishes. Please respect them and follow them.' "

Doc swallowed. Reading a letter like this was a little like discovering your own last will and testament.

" 'And so, Marty, I now say farewell and wish you Godspeed. You have been a good, kind, and loyal friend to me, and you've made—a real difference—in my life—' "

It was all too much. Doc could feel tears welling in the corners of his eyes. But he didn't want to choke up now—not when he was so close to the end of the letter.

" 'I will always treasure our relationship,' " Doc read on with a sniffle, " 'and think on you with fond memories, warm feelings, and a special place in my heart.

" 'Your friend in time, "Doc" Emmett L. Brown. September first, 1885.' "

He looked up at Marty as he wiped a tear from his eye.

"I never knew I could write anything so touching."

"I know, Doc," Marty replied, trying hard to keep his lower lip from quivering. "It's—beautiful."

It was a touching moment. Even Doc's loyal dog began to whimper.

Doc glanced down at Man's Best Friend. "It's all right, Copernicus. Everything's going to be fine." If only he felt as confident as he sounded. The letter shook in his hand. He simply couldn't understand how he could have been so careless as to allow an error of this magnitude to occur!

"I'm sorry, Doc!" Marty blurted. "It's all my fault you're stuck back there!" The teenager's hands balled into fists as he remembered whatever it was that had happened. "If only I hadn't been late!"

Doc shook his head, half to let Marty know things weren't as bad as they seemed, half to ward off the teenager telling him anything else about the future of Doctor Emmett L. Brown.

"Well," he said reassuringly, "there are plenty worse places to be than the old west. What if I'd ended up in the Dark Ages?" He laughed ruefully. "They would have probably burned me at the stake as a heretic or a warlock or something."

He fixed Marty with his best scientific gaze. "Let's see the map."

Marty handed over the other yellowed piece of paper that had been in that ancient envelope. It only took Doc a moment to decipher the map's meaning—after all, he was very well acquainted with the man who had drawn this.

Doc pointed a finger at a spot circled on the map. "According to this, the time vehicle's been sealed off in a side tunnel."

But how to get to it? Doc nodded grimly, his decision made.

"We may have to blast."

Marty's mouth fell open, as well it should. Dynamite wasn't child's play. But, as dramatic as this solution was, it was also necessary.

After all, this was all in the name of science!

•Chapter Two•

Marty plugged his ears.

Doc twisted the detonator.

The dynamite roared like the loudest, closest clap of thunder Marty had ever heard. He almost stumbled as the ground shook beneath his sneakers. A wall of dirt and bits of rock and brush rained down on top of them.

Marty threw an arm across his face. Doc had calculated that they would be safe here, a hundred yards from the blast. Safe, maybe. Clean, never.

Marty opened his eyes as the dirt stopped falling. When the dust cleared, he saw that almost half the hill was gone!

Doc may have overdone the dynamite a bit. Marty was glad that all of them—even Copernicus—were wearing miner helmets.

"I think you woke the dead with that blast," Marty shouted over his ringing ears.

But Doc shook his head impatiently.

"Just a few tombstones." He waved vaguely at the ancient graveyard on the far side of the road, where a few of the brittle old markers actually had fallen. "We'll set 'em up later."

Doc pointed in the passenger seat of their rented tow truck. "Bring that camera. I want to document this excavation—for a record!"

Marty grabbed the large flash camera and the duffel bag full of tools and supplies from the Hill Valley Army/Navy Store. Doc grabbed his own duffel bag and led the way toward the hole they had blown in the hill.

There, at the center of the new hole, was a tunnel leading into the hill and down. As they got closer, Marty saw it was a real mining tunnel, the ceiling supported by what looked like old railroad ties, with a pair of narrow railroad tracks running down into the darkness.

Doc dug a lantern out of his duffel bag and told Marty to do the same.

Doc flicked on his lantern and shined the light into the recesses where the midmorning sun didn't reach. After a quick examination to determine that the explosion hadn't harmed the support beams, Doc led the way into the tunnel. Marty turned on his own lantern, then bent down to flick on the light on Copernicus's helmet. Marty and the dog followed the eager Doc's lead.

"I've gotta hand it to myself," the inventor muttered appreciatively, "hiding the time vehicle in a location like this. The temperature stays constant, very little humidity—a perfect preservation environment. Brilliant!" Doc chuckled.

A clump of dirt fell from the ceiling, barely missing Marty's nose. He just hoped these old wooden beams were as solid as Doc thought they were. Even the dog didn't seem to be particularly comfortable in this underground tunnel. Copernicus whimpered softly, walking very close behind Marty's heels.

"This reminds me of the time I attempted to reach the center of the earth," Doc continued happily. "I'd been reading my favorite author: Jules Verne. I spent weeks preparing that expedition, and I didn't even get *this* far." He sighed wistfully. "Of course, I was only twelve at the time . . ."

Doc lifted the map into the lantern's light.

"Hmm. According to this, it should be around here—"

Marty scratched the hair under his helmet. The tunnel didn't look any different here than it had on the way down, just one more or less straight passageway leading deeper into the ground, without side tunnels or anything else particularly interesting. Unless—

Marty swung his lantern back toward one of the side beams. He could have sworn he saw something on the wood.

"Doc! Look!"

There it was, carved into the beam, three letters:

E.L.B.

"My initials!" Doc shouted. "Just like in *Journey to the Center of the Earth*. It must be right through this wall!"

Marty lifted the camera and took a flash picture. He placed the camera and new snapshot carefully into his duffel bag, then turned to help Doc remove the pile of rocks and timbers that the 1885 Doc had used to hide the DeLorean.

Doc called out excitedly. He had broken through the false wall, to show a large, open space on the other side. Marty shoved a whole pile of debris aside as Doc knocked rocks out of the way with the base of his lantern. In a matter of seconds, they had opened a space large enough for them to step through.

Doc led the way again, with Marty and Copernicus on his heels. Marty lifted his lantern next to Doc's.

There, in the middle of the chamber, was a large, low shape covered by animal skins and raised above the floor on what looked like railroad ties.

Doc and Marty grinned at each other. Without a word, the two of them pulled away the old animal hides. The DeLorean was underneath, its sleek, silver finish shining in the lantern light.

"And it's been buried here for seventy years, two months and thirteen days!" Doc exclaimed in wonder. "Astounding!"

Marty grabbed the camera and took another flash photo.

Doc leaned close to the car. The metal seemed unharmed by the car's long stay underground, but when he touched a tire, the rubber cracked beneath his fingers, flaking off and crumbling into dust.

So the car had really been here since 1885? Marty had to admit, this was really strange.

"Say, Doc," he asked, "when you uncover something that hasn't been invented yet, is it still considered archaeology?"

The inventor considered Marty's question for a second, then shook his head.

"No. Insanity."

He opened the door on the driver's side and lifted his lantern to look inside.

"Look! Another letter!"

He pulled the yellowed envelope from the car for Marty to see. Written on the paper, in Doc's bold handwriting, were the words: REPAIR INSTRUCTIONS.

This was science?

Doc held the tiny ceramic object in front of him, examining it as best he could in the lantern light. Not that there was much to examine; a melted blob that didn't mean much of anything to an inventor with a background based solidly in 1955. He was perplexed, but he was thrilled as well. So much was going to change in the next thirty years, and Doc Emmett L. Brown was going to be there to see it all, and even invent something to help it along!

Behind him, Marty read the explanatory letter aloud:

" 'As you can see, the lightning bolt shorted

out the time circuit microchip. The attached schematic diagram will allow you to build a replacement unit with 1955 components—' "

Marty passed Doc a long, rolled-up piece of paper that had been sitting in the car next to the letter. Doc unrolled the scrolled instructions and looked them over quickly. Yes, his future—or rather, past—self knew just what he needed. Now here was something he could understand!

He glanced at the charred metal bit in his hand a final time. "Unbelievable, that this little piece of nothing can be such a big problem." He looked up at Marty with a frown. "And what's it called again?"

"A microchip," Marty replied with a grin. He went back to reading the letter.

" 'But most importantly, the time display mechanism must be repaired. Otherwise, it will be impossible to set a destination time. This is a simple repair, requiring a few flashlight bulbs and some penlight batteries.' "

It was Marty's turn to frown. "Now, that's unbelievable! You end up stuck in 1885 because you can't get a few lousy flashlight bulbs."

Doc raised his hands to wave away Marty's objections.

"I wish you'd quit saying 'stuck in 1885,' Marty. Why, when I was a boy, I always wanted to be a cowboy." Heck. He remembered it still. He could feel the horse and saddle underneath him. "I even spent a few summers working at Statler's ranch." His hands curled, gripping imaginary reins. "Learned how to ride and shoot and rope . . ."

Marty got the oddest look on his face. He was probably trying to imagine Doc Brown as a cowboy.

"So how'd you end up as a scientist?" the teenager asked.

Doc grinned. He remembered this even better.

"When I was eleven years old, I read *Twenty Thousand Leagues Under the Sea* by Jules Verne, and I discovered *science!* It was the writings of Jules Verne that inspired me to become an inventor.

"Besides"—Doc shrugged—"Mr. Statler sold the ranch and went into the used-car business, so I decided there wasn't much future in cowpunching."

He paused and sighed.

"But now, knowing I'm going to spend my future in the past—that sounds like a wonderful way to spend my retirement years!"

Marty grinned back at him, convinced at last. "Doc, if you're happy, then I'm happy. It'll be a whole lot easier for me to go back to 1985, knowing you're living it up in 1885."

That sounded good to Doc, too. Now all they had to do was get the DeLorean in working order again, and all their problems would be over.

Marty had never expected it would be this much work.

The DeLorean was a sports car—actually, it was one of the ultimate, cool sports cars—so it was fairly lightweight as cars went. That meant it only weighed a ton or two; a ton that was awfully tough to maneuver when the rubber tires were so old and dry that they shredded every time they moved. Still, somehow, Doc and Marty moved it, after backing the small tow truck down into the tunnel, then using Doc's knowledge of levers and other simple machines to turn the DeLorean enough so they could then use the cable and winch to lift it for a tow. After that, all they had to do was pull the car from the tunnel, and, using what fragments of the tires that remained, push the car onto that same flatbed trailer Doc had used in his so-called lightning experiment the other night at the courthouse.

It had taken hours. Night had fallen, and Marty still had to set up the fallen tombstones.

"It just occurred to me, Marty," Doc mused as he threw a tarpaulin over the DeLorean. "Since I end up in 1885, perhaps I'm now in the history books. I wonder—could I go to the library and look myself up in the old newspaper archives?"

Marty looked up as he pushed one of the old slabs back into place. He had to put his back and shoulder into it, too—these old slate stones were heavy!

"Doc," he answered hesitantly, "you've always said it's not a good idea to know too much about your own destiny and all . . ."

Doc considered Marty's reply for a moment, then shrugged, apparently satisfied.

"You're right, Marty. I know too much already.

Better that I not attempt to uncover the circumstances of my own—er—future."

He clapped his hands, looking past Marty to his faithful dog.

"Copernicus! C'mon, boy!"

But the dog didn't budge. Copernicus looked up at Marty and whimpered.

"I'll get him, Doc!" Marty stood up. "Copernicus! C'mon, fella! We're going home!"

But the dog only sat down in front of a tombstone and whimpered again.

"What's wrong, Copernicus?" Marty called as he walked toward him.

The dog shifted from paw to paw and waved his muzzle toward the tombstone to his side. Marty had never seen the dog behave this way before. Copernicus stood up on all fours again, tail wagging. He barked assertively, like he was trying to get Marty to pay attention. This dog was acting just like those reruns of *Lassie* Marty used to watch when he was little.

Was Copernicus trying to tell Marty something?

Marty frowned. That was crazy. But, then again, any pet of Doc Brown's was bound to be one smart dog.

The dog's helmet light shone on the tombstone.

Marty glanced at the writing. He felt as though his heart was going to stop.

Oh, no, he thought. Not that.

Anything but that.

•Chapter Three•

Marty read it again. It was all there, carved in stone:

HERE LIES
EMMETT BROWN.
Date of Birth—Unknown.
Died—September 7, 1885.

And then, in smaller letters, farther down the stone:

Shot in the back by Buford Tannen
over a matter of 80 dollars.

Then, at the very bottom of the marker:

Erected in eternal memory
by his beloved Clara.

Marty swore under his breath. Shot in the back by Buford Tannen? In 1885? But the date on the tombstone was only a few days after the date on the letter Doc had sent him!

That meant, when Doc thought he was just about to settle down in the old west, he was really about to die!

Marty looked back toward the waiting tow truck. Should he tell Doc? After all, the inventor had warned him about this sort of thing—all that paradox business.

But Doc was his friend, in 1985, 1955, or 1885. He had to tell him!

"Doc!" he yelled. "Hurry!"

Doc started to amble over in Marty's direction. He hurried up, though, once he had gotten close enough to look at the teenager's face.

"Marty, what's wrong?" Doc called. "You look like you've seen a ghost!"

Marty shook his head. "You're not far off, Doc—"

He pointed at the face of the tombstone, and Doc turned to look.

"GREAT SCOTT!"

The inventor clutched his heart and staggered back. This time, though, he didn't faint. Marty wondered if Doc was getting used to all these shocks.

The inventor looked down at the ground. He made a small upset sort of sound in the back of his throat and walked backward a half-dozen very rapid paces.

Marty realized Doc had been standing on his own grave.

The inventor hugged his shoulders. "I'm getting chills." He stopped and frowned at the teenager.

"Marty, please—don't stand there."

Oh, yeah. Marty was standing on the grave, too. He quickly stepped to one side. "Sorry."

Doc waved the teen's apology aside as he re-read the tombstone.

"Shot in the back? What kind of a future is that? And who's this 'Clara'? There's no mention of any Clara in my letter."

"Maybe you found a girl friend back there," Marty suggested helpfully. "A man could get mighty lonely back in the old west."

But Marty's suggestion seemed to upset Doc even more than the gravestone. "I can't get in-volved with some pioneer woman!" the inventor exclaimed passionately. "That kind of thing could do irreparable damage to the entire space-time continuum!"

Doc took a moment to collect himself, then spoke in a calmer voice: "Better take a photo-graph, Marty. This calls for further research."

Marty dutifully took the picture. He had to run to catch up to Doc, already halfway to the tow truck. He had never seen the inventor so grim, so determined.

Marty couldn't blame him, though. This time, it was Doc's future that was at stake.

Great Scott! The answer was probably right un-der his nose!

Of course, until now, Doc Brown hadn't even realized there was a question.

The City Archives, down in the basement of the Hill Valley City Hall, would have been long closed by the time they towed the DeLorean back to safety. And they would have stayed closed, too, if Doc hadn't known Charlie the night watchman. Charlie and Doc both shared a passion for the old west in general, and the history of Hill Valley in particular—and Charlie could be talked into bending the rules a little when it came to visiting hours and suchlike, especially if you shared some of the history you found.

So Doc had brought Marty into the file room, a place filled with bound newspapers, local memorabilia, and dozens of cabinets filled with old photos and clippings about the region. There was really almost too much information down here. You could spend days down here if you didn't know exactly what you were looking for. But Doc hoped they could find everything they needed in the file drawer marked "Hill Valley: 1880s."

They hadn't found any mention yet of any "Emmett Browns," but there was other information about the local past that Doc found rather disquieting.

Marty read a particularly disturbing passage aloud:

" 'Buford Tannen was a notorious gunman, whose short temper earned him the nickname "Mad Dog." He was quick on the trigger, and bragged that he had killed twelve men, not including Indians or Chinamen.' "

Doc glanced over Marty's shoulder. There, in the file Marty had pulled from the drawer, was a photograph of "Mad Dog" Tannen. He looked awfully familiar. Doc realized the gunfighter bore a striking resemblance to Biff Tannen, a local teenager who had had more than one run-in with Marty over the past couple of days. Could Mad Dog be Biff's great-grandfather? It was certainly within the realm of scientific possibility.

Still, Doc reminded himself, Biff's parentage wasn't the central issue here. They were looking for historical references to one Emmett L. Brown.

"Is there any mention of me?" Doc asked Marty. "Was I one of the twelve?"

Marty kept on reading:

" 'However, this claim cannot be substantiated since precise records were not kept after Tannen shot a newspaper editor who printed an unfavorable story about him in 1884.' "

He looked up at Doc and shrugged. "I guess that's why we can't find anything."

Doc turned his attention to a file of his own and came to somebody else who looked familiar—a man, in his mid-twenties who bore a resemblance to Marty. The picture came from the early 1900s, a little later than what they were looking for, but the man was surrounded by his family, including an older man—his father, perhaps?—who was dressed as a farmer.

"Look," Doc pointed out. " 'William McFly and family.' Your relatives?"

Marty nodded. "Yeah. I think my great-grandfather was named William—" He glanced at the photo. "Nice-looking fella."

The teenager paused to look again at the photo they had taken of the tombstone.

"Maybe it's a mistake, Doc, and it's really not your grave. Maybe there was another Emmett Brown in 1885. Did you have any relatives here back then?"

Doc could only wish that were true. "No," he replied. "The Browns didn't move to Hill Valley until 1908, and then they were the Von Brauns. My father changed it during World War One."

Marty went back to flipping through the file in front of him.

They both stared at the next photograph, open-mouthed. There couldn't be any doubt anymore.

The caption read: THE NEW CLOCK, SEPTEMBER 5, 1885.

And in the photo stood the white-haired "Doc" Emmett L. Brown, dressed in a long coat and tie, western boots, and a Stetson hat, right next to a six-foot-high clock face resting on top of a Conestoga wagon.

Doc felt a sinking feeling inside his Hawaiian shirt.

"Great Scott! It's me! Then it is true! All of it. It is me who goes back there and gets shot." He looked up to his teenaged friend. "What's the date on that letter?"

Marty reached inside his jacket pocket and pulled out the crumpled yellow letter.

"September first, 1885," he read again.

Doc swallowed as he took the letter from

Marty. Every additional fact felt—quite literally—like another nail in his coffin.

"That means—" he said slowly but firmly—there was, after all, no denying the truth—his death was history! "—I get killed a week after I write the letter."

Marty lifted his gaze from the book and looked straight into the inventor's eyes.

"No, Doc," the teenager announced solemnly. "None of that's gonna happen, because I'm gonna go back to 1885 and bring you home."

Great Scott! Marty was going to go back into the past? But wouldn't that change history? What if the teenager somehow created another paradox?

Then again, come to think about it, the fact that Doc Brown had ended up in the past had changed history already, hadn't it? After all, Doc was there in the history books! If Marty rescued him from the past, would history go back to the way it had been before? And—for that matter—was there really any way to know?

It was really too bad Doc couldn't travel back there himself—but having two Doc Browns in the past, where neither one of them belonged, invited far more paradoxes than the inventor cared to think about. In fact, the more he considered this, the more confusing this time travel business became. He sighed. In the true and final analysis, Doc Brown only wanted to know one thing:

Could Marty pull this off?

•Chapter Four•

Wednesday, November 16, 1955
9:55 A.M.

Marty saw nothing but Indians.

Sure, this place was called the "Pohatchee Drive-In," after the Indians who used to live around Hill Valley, but Marty thought the designers of this particular outdoor movie theater might have gone a little overboard. Besides the neon Indian on the marquee out front, everything—from the concession booth to the base of the movie screen—was painted with teepees, arrows, and lots and lots of Indians.

Marty supposed the folks who built this place needed some sort of gimmick to get the crowds way out here. The Pohatchee Drive-In was a good forty minutes from the middle of town.

And that, come to think of it, was another problem.

"It's gonna be some walk back to Hill Valley

from here." Especially, Marty thought, if he had to wear these too-tight cowboy boots!

But Doc wasn't about to change his mind. "It's still the safest plan. After all, we can't risk sending you back into a populated area, or to a spot that's geographically unknown. You don't want to crash into some tree that once existed in the past."

Doc waved at the spectacular rock formations around them. "This area was completely open country. And since where you are going there are no roads, this terrain is safe to drive across. You'll have plenty of run-out space when you arrive."

He turned away from the movie screen and pointed at what looked like a small cave beyond the concession stand.

"Now," Doc explained, "there's a cave back there which will be a perfect place to hide the time vehicle."

Marty walked a few paces closer to the cave to get a better look. The ditch appeared to be about five feet deep, and Doc was right, there was some sort of cave at the far end.

Marty pushed his new, blindingly white cowboy hat back off his forehead.

"The clothes fit?" Doc asked.

Marty nodded unenthusiastically. "All except the boots. They're too tight."

He held up the offending footwear. He had tried them on, but had gone back to his Nikes when the boots had crushed his toes. There was another problem here, too. Even though the other stuff fit, he wasn't too sure about this elaborate pink-and-blue shirt. Not only did the yellow fringe get in the way, but what about that fancy design just below each shoulder—didn't those elaborate circles look an awful lot like exploding atoms? Marty didn't even think they had atoms in 1885. And did cowboys wear this kind of elaborately tooled golden sunburst belt? What the heck, the buckle was almost as big as one of his shoes!

He had to ask. "Now, are you sure this stuff is authentic, Doc? I mean, Clint Eastwood never wore anything like this."

Doc frowned.

"Clint who?"

Whoops. Marty had forgotten. Clint Eastwood wouldn't start making westerns until the sixties.

"Oh, right," he explained. "You don't know him yet."

But Doc wouldn't be sidetracked. He pointed down at Marty's sneakers.

"Marty, you'll have to wear the boots, even if they are uncomfortable. You can't wear those futuristic things in 1885. You shouldn't even be wearing them in 1955."

The only thing Marty could think of was the way the boots pinched his toes. He hated to give up a pair of sneakers. Once you broke in a pair of shoes—

Still, he didn't want to have anything go wrong with his rescue of Doc.

"I'll put 'em on when I get there," he promised.

He looked out over the wide-open prairie. It was

just beginning to sink in—he was going back to visit the wild west!

"Hey, Doc," he asked, "you think I'll get a chance to ride a horse? I used to ride at summer camp. I was pretty good, too."

Doc smiled at that.

"I don't see why not." He glanced back at the car. "I think that's everything. Your other clothes are packed. I put gas in the tank. What about the hoverboard device?"

Oh, yeah. They couldn't forget that. Marty reached into the back of Doc's Packard.

"Right here." He tucked the pink thing under the DeLorean's passenger seat. Not that he would use something like that in the old west, except maybe as a last resort. But the hoverboard didn't belong in 1955, and Marty couldn't stand to see it destroyed. So it came with him—once he'd rescued Doc from the old west—back to 1985.

"And you mustn't forget the photographic evidence," Doc added hurriedly. He passed Marty the photo of Doc at the clock tower they had taken from the archives and the snapshot showing Doc's grave. "If you have any trouble convincing me to come back with you, just show me these."

"Right," Marty replied. He paused and frowned in at the mass of wires and vacuum tubes that now was mounted on the hood of the DeLorean. That, and the big fifties-style tires that Doc had mounted on the car to replace the ones that had shredded with age, made the DeLorean look like one of those so-called funny cars Marty used to see when he went down to the Hill Valley Speed-way.

He glanced back at Doc. "You're sure this thing'll work?"

"Of course!" the inventor responded enthusiastically. "This device will do everything that—uh—'microchip' could do." He paused to scratch his head. "I would have made it bigger, but there wasn't room."

Doc stuck a hand over the glowing tubes.

"Well, the tubes are warmed up—"

He opened the door to the DeLorean and climbed into the car.

"Time circuits on—" he added as he twisted the appropriate handle.

"Destination time—" Doc pulled the letter from his pocket. "I wrote the letter on September first, so we'll send you back to the very next day—September second—that's a Wednesday."

Doc punched the new date on the DeLorean's key pad:

DESTINATION TIME
SEPT. 2, 1885, 8:00 A.M.

Next to the destination were the two other time displays; where they were now:

PRESENT TIME
NOVEMBER 16, 1955, 10:00 A.M.

And, of course, the last time the machine was used.

Marty did some quick arithmetic. The machine had been sitting here since 1885. That meant these circuits—the flux capacitor and all that—hadn't been used in over seventy years!

Did Doc know what he was doing? Marty certainly hoped so.

"I get shot on Monday," Doc announced as he climbed back out of the car, "so you'll have five days to locate me. According to my letter, I'm a blacksmith, so I probably have a shop somewhere."

Marty pushed all his doubts behind him. He had a job to do.

"Don't worry, Doc," he said, perhaps a bit more confidently than he felt. "I'll find you."

Doc, perhaps sensing some of the doubts going through Marty's head, frowned down at his teenage friend.

"Marty, you don't have to do this. If you want to go back to 1985—it's all right."

But it wasn't all right. That was the one thing Marty knew for sure.

"Doc, I got you into this mess," he replied, more certain of his purpose. "I'm gonna get you out."

The inventor paused for a minute, his eyes blinking rapidly.

"Thank you," he managed at last. Doc looked like he was going to get choked up all over again.

Instead, the inventor pointed at the drive-in

movie screen. "Drive the time vehicle directly toward that screen. If you go the other way, you'll come up on that gully too fast and you might bottom out the car and rip the gas tank or fuel lines."

Marty stared at the large, white expanse at the far end of the drive-in.

"But, Doc," he objected, pointing at the wild-west mural painted beneath the expanse of white, "if I drive at the screen, I'll crash into those Indians."

But Doc shook his head in that no-nonsense scientific way of his.

"Marty, you're not thinking four-dimensionally. Temporal displacement will occur before you get to the screen. You'll instantly be transported to 1885 and those Indians won't even be there."

"Oh, right," Marty answered. They wouldn't have drive-ins in the old west. Marty wondered if he would ever really get used to time travel.

Doc reached inside the tow truck and pulled out a gunbelt, complete with a Colt revolver.

"You're sure you don't want to take this?"

It was Marty's turn to shake his head. He didn't want to use a gun.

"No, thanks. I don't know how to use it anyway."

Doc nodded and tossed the gunbelt back in the truck.

He turned and looked at Marty. This was it, then. Marty stepped forward, and the two of them hugged each other.

"Good luck," Doc said, almost choking up once again. "For both our sakes. See you—in the future."

Marty stepped back to look up at his friend.

"You mean the past."

Doc shrugged.

"Whenever."

Marty lowered himself into the DeLorean and closed the gull-wing door. He turned the key in the ignition. The engine caught and roared to life. He was on his way.

Doc knocked on the window.

Marty opened the door as Doc leaned down to speak to him.

"Marty," the inventor began hesitantly, "I know I've cautioned you about interfering in events of the past, but if for some reason you fail, and I end up getting shot in the back"—he paused and took a deep breath—"get that son of a bitch who does it."

Marty grinned up at his mentor.

"I won't fail, Doc."

He closed the door again as Doc stepped out of his path. Marty put the DeLorean in gear and turned the DeLorean across the asphalt and gravel, toward the drive-in screen.

"Happy Trails, Marty!" Doc called after him. *"Vaya con Dios!"*

Marty waved and shifted the DeLorean up through the gears. He aimed the car for center screen and floored the accelerator.

The DeLorean responded perfectly. Marty looked at the speedometer. He was up to 60—

70—80. He eased off the accelerator ever so slightly and watched it climb those last few miles per hour—84—85—86—87.

He glanced in the rearview mirror. He could see the flux capacitor start to glow.

This really *was* it.

He heard three sonic booms, saw three flashes of white light.

"Hi yo, silver," Marty whispered as he vanished into the past.

•Chapter Five•

There were Indians everywhere!

But the movie screen was gone.

The first thing Marty saw was a cloud of dust, rising from a ridge directly ahead. And then there were galloping horses, charging over the ridge, a hundred horses or more. And mounted on those horses were a hundred men, some wearing buckskin, some with feathered headdresses, some with little more than loincloths and designs painted on their chests and arms and faces. Marty recognized those clothes and designs from his high school Hill Valley history class. It was the local Indian tribe, at least local in 1885—the Pohatchees!

And all hundred of them were headed straight toward him.

What did you say at a time like this?

"INDIANS!" Marty yelled at the top of his lungs.

He hastily shifted the DeLorean into reverse.

The Pohatchee braves kept on coming. Marty could hear their war cries even over the racing car engine.

Marty swung the steering wheel to the right. He hit the brakes, threw the car into first gear, and swung the wheel to the left. The Indians were getting closer. He could make out their angry faces in his rearview mirror. Marty accelerated and shifted up to second. He was outta here!

Or maybe he wasn't.

The smooth asphalt and gravel surface of the drive-in was gone. Marty was driving the De-Lorean across open desert land, very rough, dry, bumpy, open desert land. The car's wheels lurched from a prairie dog hole to a dry wash creek bed to a rock outcropping, jarring Marty's whole body with every new obstacle. He didn't dare go any faster, for fear that he would bend a wheel rim or do some damage to the underside of the car.

Still, he told himself, he shouldn't panic. A car was faster than a horse. He was getting away, after all. He would worry about the Indians when he could see the whites of their eyes.

Marty looked out the side-view mirror. The Pohatchees were *really* close now. He could actually see the whites of their eyes, and the Indians' pupils inside the whites of their eyes, too—not to mention their rifles, knives, and bows and arrows.

He looked down at the speedometer. He was only doing fifteen miles an hour!

It was time to panic.

"Help!" Marty yelled. It was also time to put the pedal to the metal, and worry about the consequences later.

The DeLorean bounced faster and faster across the rough desert terrain, up to twenty and twenty-five, then close to thirty miles an hour. Marty risked another look out the side-view mirror. The Indians weren't gaining on him anymore, but they weren't losing ground, either.

He looked back out the front windshield. He couldn't see the ground ahead very well. The DeLorean was bouncing so much now that there was dust everywhere. It looked pretty clear ahead—no big cactuses or rock outcroppings showed through the haze. Still, he didn't like the banging noises the car was making as the tires jumped over the uneven desert ground.

He looked in the mirror again. It might have been his imagination, but the Indians looked even closer than they did before.

What would the Pohatchee do if they caught him? Marty wished he had paid more attention in those Hill Valley history classes. As he recalled, there wasn't much love lost between the Pohatchees and the local settlers, especially during the 1880s. The Indians would probably just shoot him a few times to make sure he was dead, leaving his body riddled with arrows and bullet holes. He didn't think the Pohatchee were the scalping sort. Actually, didn't he remember something from his history course about Indians learning that particular custom from the white settlers, who had scalped Indians in the first place? Well, all Marty could hope was that the Pohatchee didn't want to return the favor.

He could definitely hear their war cries now, even through the closed windows. Maybe, Marty thought, if he could just go a little faster.

The ground dropped away beneath him. Marty was slammed forward as the car stopped dead.

It took him a moment to realize he had dropped right into that gully that Doc had told him to hide the car in. Marty also realized it was a good thing he had been wearing his seat belt—otherwise, he might really have gotten hurt.

Of course, now the Indians would get him for sure. With the DeLorean's engine off, he could really hear the sound of one hundred screaming braves riding four hundred thundering hooves. The noise was deafening.

He looked out and above the windshield. The Pohatchee had reached the gully.

And then the Indians jumped over him. First one horse, then a pair, followed by dozens more, all leaping over the gully and the DeLorean, and riding away.

They just kept on going. None of them stopped. After a moment, the sound of their thundering hooves faded in the distance.

Marty got out of the car. There were the Indians, getting farther away with every second, completely ignoring him, riding into the distance until horses and riders were once again lost in a cloud of dust.

He wondered why they hadn't stopped. They had to have seen the car. Maybe they thought the DeLorean was some kind of covered wagon. Maybe the Pohatchee just had something more important to do. Whatever the reason, he supposed he should be relieved.

That's when he heard the bugle blowing "charge."

Marty looked back where the Indians had come from.

There was the United States Cavalry, a hundred mounted men strong, headed straight for him!

Marty knew what to say at a time like this:

"OH, NO!"

He jumped into the DeLorean and slammed the door after him.

A moment later, a hundred cavalry horses leapt over the gully and the DeLorean, then rode away, in pursuit of the Indians.

Apparently, nobody thought twice about this funny-looking wagon Marty had traveled here in—not as a threat, at least, or something that should turn either group away from their regular cowboy-and-Indian business.

The sounds of bugle and horses faded into the distance, too.

Marty popped open the gull-wing door and peeked out. Everything was quiet. He climbed out of the car, breathing a sigh of relief. He had ended up in the gully, where he was supposed to be in the first place. There, a few feet away in front of him, was the cave where he was supposed to hide the DeLorean. He should be able to push the car that far without any trouble. This whole thing could have been worse.

But here he was in the old west. It was time to complete his cowboy outfit. He reached into the backseat of the car and pulled out the boots. Now all he needed was a handy rock or something to sit upon to put these on.

Marty paused. What was that trickling sound? There was a familiar smell, too, that he couldn't quite place. He looked down and saw a stream of liquid coming from underneath the front of the car.

"Gas!" he muttered in disbelief. "I ripped the gas tank!"

Maybe this whole thing *was* worse after all. Still, he couldn't give up just because he saw some gasoline. The hole under the car could be tiny. There might be some way to plug the leak. Marty bent down to take a closer look.

He heard a noise from the cave behind him—a growling noise.

Marty looked over his shoulder at the cave mouth, and a rushing grizzly bear!

"Yaaaah!" Marty remarked.

The grizzly bear ran toward him.

Marty ran, too. His boots fell from his grip, but there was no time to stop and retrieve them.

Then his fancy, white, ten-gallon hat flew from his head. Too bad. Marty had a bear on his rear end—the kind of problem that only had one possible solution.

Marty ran like hell.

•Chapter
Six•

Didn't this open countryside ever end?

Marty felt like he had been walking forever. The sun had climbed up in the sky behind him, swung overhead, and now was sinking directly in his path. Doc had told him Hill Valley was due west, hadn't he? So where was it already?

It could have been worse. At least the grizzly wasn't following him. Marty had risked a look back when he had reached the top of the gully, and saw the bear had stopped to sniff the cowboy boots he'd dropped in his escape. Marty kept on going, glad for the head start, and he still wasn't going back, at least not by himself. A bear that was interested in human boots might want some human feet next.

By now, he had reached some farmland. It was the first sign of people he had seen—heck, it was first sign of just about *anything* he'd seen—since those Indians and cavalry, way back at the De-Lorean.

Marty walked cautiously between two rows of low, green plants, careful not to squash any of the greenery underfoot. He wondered if any of this stuff was good to eat. He didn't recognize it, probably because it wasn't wrapped in plastic with a grocery store label on it.

Civilization had to be around here some-where—if only he could keep walking and ignore how tired he was. It was good he had found this farmland, with its rows of vegetables. It helped him walk in a straight line.

Still, he almost stumbled once or twice in the loose earth beneath his feet. He needed food. He needed water. He needed rest. He needed to stay far away from bears. He looked down at his dust-covered sneakers. Oh, yeah. He was supposed to change into his boots, wasn't he? Those same boots that were stuck, along with his hat, back with the DeLorean, and the bear.

He reached a slight rise between two of the fields and saw buildings in the distance. But there weren't enough of them for a town, even a small wild west town like Hill Valley. There were only two small shacks. Marty guessed one was a farmhouse, the other a barn.

Marty had to admit it:

"I'm lost," he said aloud.

He squinted at the smaller of the two build-ings, the one with the smaller door, fit to let hu-mans in and out, rather than that place with the big doors for wagons and farm animals. That meant that this was the farmhouse, the other building the barn. Marty was very proud he had figured this out.

Of course, because he was staring at the buildings, how could he be expected to see the ravine? His feet, unfortunately, found the ravine for him. All of a sudden, there was no ground underneath his sneakers. He was rolling down the side of a hill, straight toward a fence somebody had stuck in his way. His head connected solidly with one of the posts.

Marty yelled out. That hurt. It was getting dark around here, too. And there were an awful lot of stars. Marty found himself flat on his back. It was nice, being on his back. It meant he didn't have to walk anymore. Maybe he should close his eyes. Maybe he would never have to walk again.

Somehow, through the darkness and the stars, Marty saw a pair of dust-covered boots.

"Maggie!" a man's voice called overhead. "Fetch some water! We've a hurt man here!"

Somehow, Marty managed to turn his head enough to look at the man kneeling over him. The fellow was wearing overalls and a workshirt, and a round hat—sort of a derby, except it was made out of straw. He was probably only a few years older than Marty, although it was hard to tell with the fellow's full red beard. But there was something more, something oddly familiar about this farmer. If only Marty could think, he knew he would put his finger on it right away.

But Marty couldn't even see straight. The heat,

the thirst, the pain in his backside, were all getting to him. Things were going in and out of focus; the farmer's concerned face, the clear, blue sky overhead, the half-built fence stretching off into the distance. Marty felt two strong hands grab him under the arms and drag him up toward the farmhouse. He tried to stay awake, to focus on the logs and dirt at the side of the door. There was a post there, and on the post a hand-carved nameplate.

Oh, no. Marty was losing it. He was hallucinating for sure.

Marty closed his eyes and let the fever take him away.

He could have sworn the nameplate read McFly.

Marty opened his eyes, but the room was dark.

He had been dreaming again. And his dreams kept getting wilder, full of Doc Brown and Clint Eastwood and the old west and who knew what else.

Marty shifted in bed. There was somebody else in the room with him—somebody he knew.

"Mom?" Marty managed, his lips dry, his voice cracking. "Is that you?"

He could see her dark silhouette as she leaned over him. She wiped his forehead with a cool, damp cloth.

"There, there now," she said softly. "You've been asleep for nearly half a day now."

Marty let out a sigh of relief. His mother's voice made everything seem safe and sound. But why was she speaking with an Irish accent? Marty decided to ignore it. It probably had something to do with his fever.

"Ohh," he groaned instead. "I had a horrible nightmare. I dreamt I was in this western, and these Indians were chasing me—"

"Well," his mother's voice interrupted reassuringly, "you're safe and sound here at the McFly farm."

Marty blinked.

"McFly farm?"

Marty sat up as his mother struck a match and lit an oil lamp.

Except it wasn't his mother—was it?

The woman had sat in a chair at the side of the bed. She was in her early twenties, and wore a dark blue, flowered dress and a white apron. Her long brown hair was pinned up behind her head in a bun. She still looked an awful lot like Marty's mother.

Except—Marty remembered this now—he had gone back in the DeLorean to the old west.

"You're—" Marty began. But she wasn't.

"You're my—" he tried again. Then who would she be?

"Who are you?" he asked at last.

The woman who was not his mother smiled sweetly.

"The name's McFly. Maggie McFly."

"Maggie—McFly?" Marty replied uncertainly. So they were related after all. Was that why she looked so much like his mother?

"And that's Missus McFly," Maggie chided

gently, "and don't you be forgettin' the 'Missus.'"

Marty looked away, realizing he had been staring at her. He cleared his throat. He didn't know what to say to this woman who wasn't his mother.

"And what might be your name, sir?" Missus Maggie McFly asked in that same gentle voice.

His name? Well, that was easy enough.

"Uh, Mc—" Marty stopped himself. These folks were his relatives—great-great-grandparents or something. He couldn't possibly tell them who he really was. It might cause one of those paradoxes Doc Brown was always warning about.

But what could he call himself? Marty chose the first name that popped into his head:

"Uh, Eastwood. Clint Eastwood."

Maggie nodded pleasantly to acknowledge the introduction. She gently patted Marty's head.

"You've a bump on the noggin, Mr. Eastwood, but not too serious. You'll be sore, but I think it'll be healin' all right."

Marty gently brushed against the spot where his head had met the fence post. Ouch. Marty had never realized wood could be that hard.

"Although," Maggie went on, "I am curious about your garments—most peculiar they are."

His clothes—was there something wrong with them after all? He should never have let Doc talk him into wearing this stuff—unless, of course, she was talking about his sneakers. He decided it was time to change the subject.

"What day is it?" he asked. "How long have I been out?"

"It's Wednesday evening. You've—been out"— Maggie said the words like the expression was new to her—"a few hours."

She passed a steaming cup of something to Marty.

"This'll help clear your head, bring down your fever."

Marty gingerly accepted the cup from her, careful to hold it by the handle. He wondered what the cup held. Coffee, maybe. Probably, though, it was some sort of herbal tea—a good, old-fashioned western remedy.

"Lucky for you," Maggie added, "Seamus found you when he did."

"Seamus?" Marty asked as he brought the cup up to his lips.

"My husband, Seamus McFly," Maggie explained. "He's out getting supper."

Marty sipped his tea.

It wasn't tea. He almost gagged. He felt like his eyes were going to leap out of his head. This stuff must be a hundred proof!

"Tasty, isn't it?" Maggie remarked pleasantly. "An old Irish recipe. We make it ourselves."

A baby started to cry in some other part of the house.

Maggie stood quickly, her hands smoothing the wrinkles from her apron. "Ah, you'll be excusin' me, Mr. Eastwood, while I tend to the little one."

Marty nodded. "The little one. Right."

Maggie was already out of the room. She closed the door behind her.

Marty put the steaming liquor down on the bedside table. It might be an old family recipe, but he didn't have time to get drunk on it. He had to save Doc Brown from being shot in the back, and he had already lost the better part of a day between walking and being unconscious. He quickly put on his underwear, then his pants, as he took a quick look around the bedroom. It was small, with a dirt floor, crammed with a half-dozen pieces of handmade furniture. It looked comfortable enough, though, in its way, for the guest bedroom.

Marty opened the door and walked into the next room. This room was full of things, too; a cradle, a spinning wheel, a dinner table and chairs, a wood stove with a boiling kettle on top. The place seemed a combination living-dining-workroom with a kitchen thrown in. There was one other door in this room, which was open to let in light. He could tell from a glance at the deep blue evening sky that that door led outside.

Oh. He realized that the room he'd just walked out of wasn't the guest bedroom—it was the only bedroom. And the bedroom and this room made up the entire farmhouse. Maybe this frontier farm life was tougher than Marty thought.

Maggie stood by the cradle, rocking a baby in her arms. The baby's crying was softer now, and stopped now and then for the infant to catch its breath.

Maggie smiled at Marty as he walked closer.

"This here is William Sean McFly. Aged five months. He's the first of our family to be born in America." She glanced down at the baby. "It's all right, Will. This is Mr. Clint Eastwood here, visitin'."

The baby looked up at Marty and smiled.

"Sure'n he likes you, Mr. Eastwood," Maggie said.

There was a sizzling noise from the stove behind them. Marty glanced around to see that the pot was boiling over.

"Oh, Lord!" Maggie took a step toward the stove. She glanced down at William Sean, then thrust him into Marty's arms. "Hold him a moment, Mr. Eastwood, while I tend to that."

Marty looked down at the baby as Maggie rushed to the stove.

"Hi, there, fella," he said softly. "Hiya, Will." He wasn't too sure how to hold a baby, especially as important a baby as this one. Will didn't seem to mind, though. He was still smiling.

"You must be my great-grandfather," Marty continued, almost overwhelmed by it all. The chance to meet your frontier ancestors! It was—cosmic. Marty could barely manage to speak his thoughts aloud. "The first McFly of America—"

Except what was that smell? And why did his knee feel wet? Marty looked down.

"—and you peed on me," he concluded.

Before Marty could reflect on the cosmic significance of all this, Seamus showed up, a shotgun in one hand, a pair of dead jackrabbits in the other.

"I got supper!" he announced as he slammed the door behind him.

Jackrabbits? Well, Marty supposed he was hungry enough to try just about anything. Wasn't rabbit supposed to taste like chicken, anyway?

Marty sighed. He hoped he could find Doc soon.

Supper was ready at last. And, Marty had to admit, he was ready for it. The smells that had come from the stew pot in the last hour or so had convinced him how hungry he really was. Stewed rabbit was beginning to sound like one of the best meals Marty had ever had.

Little Will had fallen back asleep, and the three adults all sat down at the dinner table, a plate heaped with rabbit and vegetables in front of each of them. Marty reached quickly for his knife and fork.

He hesitated when he saw Seamus's folded hands.

"From thy bounty through Christ Our Lord, Amen," Seamus said reverently.

"Amen," Maggie chorused.

"Amen," Marty added hastily as Seamus and Maggie crossed themselves. He had forgotten all about people saying grace. He looked down at his plate. Maybe he'd better wait and see what the others did before he started to eat.

Both Seamus and Maggie picked up their forks and knives. Marty couldn't think of a better invitation. He carved out a hunk of rabbit and took a hearty bite. It wasn't bad either; a little bit like chick—

Something in his mouth went crack.

"Careful," Seamus cautioned. "There still might be some buckshot in there."

Marty reached into his mouth and pulled out a small, black pellet. He smiled weakly.

"How about some nice well water, Mr. Eastwood?" Maggie asked as she picked up a pitcher.

That sounded safe enough, Marty decided. Water might help wash out any left over buckshot, too.

"Thanks," Marty agreed.

She poured some water into his glass—except it looked more like mud than water, or maybe really weak chocolate milk. When you got well water, Marty realized, you got some of the well, too.

Seamus interrupted Marty's contemplation of the mud-filled glass with a question: "So, if you don't mind me askin', Mr. Eastwood, what's your trade?"

"My trade?" Marty asked. He didn't quite understand. Was Seamus asking him about his experience in swapping things?

"By the condition of your hands," Seamus explained, "it's clear that you ain't a farmer or a lumberman or a miner. I've only seen hands like that on a gambler or a baby, and sure'n you ain't no baby."

Oh. His trade. Like, in a job. Marty looked back down at his dirty water glass. He couldn't tell them the truth. *Oh, I'm just your average high school student, Mr. McFly, except that I like to travel through time.* Marty looked back up at the McFlys. Well, maybe he could, sort of.

"No," Marty replied, "actually, I'm still in school."

Seamus looked at him in disbelief. "School? At your age?"

Maggie frowned at her husband. "Where exactly do you come from, Mr. Eastwood?" she asked, gently changing the subject.

Marty hoped he could answer this question better than he had the last one. "Well, actually, I'm—from around here—originally. But I've been sort of traveling. For a long time—years." Marty decided this might be a good time to change the subject all over again.

"And you guys are from Ireland?"

"Aye," Seamus replied with a grin. "Ballybowhill."

Ballybowwhich? Marty had never heard of the place. Then again, he guessed he hadn't heard of much outside of Dublin. Ballybowhill. It had a nice ring to it.

"We married there," Seamus explained, "but came to America in hopes of a better life. To own some land, have a place of our own, with room to grow. That's my dream. Sure'n I think we've finally found it here in Hill Valley."

"Aye," Maggie chimed in brightly, glad, Marty guessed, they were on a topic that the two of them agreed upon, "we're gettin' to be a right fine growin' community, what with the railroad here now, and the new courthouse goin' up. And our festival this Saturday night, why that'll be a cel-

ebration to make anyone proud." She smiled at
Marty. "Is that what brings you here, Mr. Eastwood?"

A festival on Saturday? Well, if he couldn't
find Doc before that, surely the inventor would
show up at something like that—all the townspeople would. But Doc was going to be shot on
the next Monday. That would only give them two
days until—Marty didn't want to think about it.
Instead, he tried to answer Maggie's question,
and this one he could answer—more or less—
truthfully.

"No, actually, I came to visit an old friend of
mine. He's a blacksmith. Maybe you know him—
his name's Brown."

"Brown?" Seamus answered with a frown.
"Aye, he's that strange fella, kinda drifted into
town beginning of the year. Don't know much
about him, except he set up shop in the old livery
stable in town."

So Doc really was here, and probably only a
couple miles away. The sooner Marty got going,
the better. He stood up and took a step toward
the door.

"Which way is town?" he asked. "I gotta
find—"

He stopped suddenly, realizing he had to do
something else first.

"Uh, listen," he asked somewhat more tenta-
tively, "could I—use the bathroom?"

"The which?" Maggie asked politely.

"The bathroom," Marty repeated. With all the

heat and the well water, Marty needed to use it now.

" 'Bath room'?" Seamus asked with one of his all-too-frequent frowns. "I'm confused by what you're saying, sir. If it's a bath you be wantin', well, the stream's about a third a mile yonder, but I'd suggest you wait 'til morning."

Oh, no, Marty thought. What would they call it in 1885?

"Actually no," he tried again. "I just need to take a—uh, relieve myself."

"Then why didn't you say so the first time?" Seamus asked. "Sure'n, we have a privy! It's in the back."

Oh, thank goodness, Marty thought. In the back? He didn't remember seeing one back there. Still, he probably just hadn't looked hard enough.

"Bath room?" Seamus remarked, half to his wife, half to himself. "Curious turn of a phrase. Sure'n it don't make much sense."

Marty started quickly for the bedroom.

"Excuse me," Seamus remarked rather loudly, "but where do you think you're goin'?"

Marty stopped. This was getting serious. Maybe if he crossed his legs—

"Didn't you say it was in the back?" he asked, trying to keep the desperation from his voice.

"Aye." Seamus nodded. "Outside. Whatever would possess you to think we'd have it inside our home? And next to where we sleep, yet?"

Oh. Of course.

"It's outside." It was Marty's turn to nod his

head. This was 1885, after all. "Right. An out-house. Sorry, my mistake."

He turned and walked as quickly as he was able from the house.

Oh, dear. This was troublesome. They were good Christian folk and all, but perhaps, this time, their generosity had gone too far.

Maggie turned to her husband. From the look on Seamus's face, she could tell he was thinking exactly the same thing.

"I hope we ain't brought a curse on us takin' him in," Maggie blurted. "Plain to see he's feeble-minded." She thought again about that fancy shirt with the pearl buttons and those odd shoes. "And the Lord only knows how he came by those things he's wearin'."

Seamus nodded and smiled at her. My, but she still liked the way that man smiled.

"Aye, he's a bit strange," her husband agreed, "but I got a sort of feelin' about him—can't quite understand it, but that, well, that it's important that we look after him."

That was her husband, an optimist, and a man of faith. And, Lord knew, this Mr. Eastwood might be simple, but he certainly didn't look like he could do any harm. If her husband thought they should look after the fellow, that was good enough for her. After all, she knew when they came to America that things would be a bit different from Ireland.

Still, she never expected them to be quite this different.

•Chapter Seven•

It couldn't get any worse than this.

Marty burst out of the outhouse. He had never smelled anything so foul in his entire life! At least he'd been able to relieve himself, but he'd had to do it holding his breath! Whoa! If all the facilities were like this around here, he would have to learn to use bushes or something for the rest of his stay in 1885. Of course, he wasn't going to stay here any longer than he absolutely had to. That was one thing he decided while he was holding his breath.

He walked around to the front of the house.

"Mr. and Mrs. McFly!" he called in through the front door. "Listen, I really appreciate everything you've done, taking care of me and all, but if you could just tell me how to get to town from here, so I can find the Doc—uh, the blacksmith."

There was silence inside the farmhouse. Marty took a step inside. Maggie and Seamus looked at each other as if Marty had just said the dumbest thing in the world. Seamus looked back at Marty.

"Surely," he said slowly, as if afraid Marty might not understand, "you're not considerin' settin' out for town now."

Well, Seamus was right. Marty didn't understand.

"Why not?" he asked.

"It's dark," Seamus explained.

But Marty didn't understand the explanation. Well, he guessed it might be dangerous out here in the dark, with Indians and outlaws and all. No streetlights either.

"Right," he answered, not really convinced.

"There's wolves out at night here, Mr. Eastwood," Maggie added. "And bears."

Oh. Wolves? Bears? Marty nodded. He knew darn well there were bears. Not just outlaws and Indians, but wolves and bears?

"Right." Now Marty was convinced.

Perhaps, he considered, he should stay the night after all.

"Mr. Eastwood," Seamus suggested, "why don't you sleep here tonight, and tomorrow—well, I can't take you all the way into town, but I'll take you as far as the railroad tracks, and you can follow them to town."

That was awfully nice of them. But Marty didn't want to be a bother.

"Hey, look," he said, "I don't want to put you out. I'll walk. No problem."

"Sure'n he can walk," Maggie agreed. "It's only fourteen miles."

Marty looked at Mrs. McFly.

"Did you say fourteen miles?"

He could feel his feet ache already.

Thursday, September 3, 1885

Marty waved good-bye to his great-great-grandfather.

"—and thanks for the hat!"

He took off the slightly battered straw derby that Seamus had insisted Marty keep to protect his head from the sun. He waved the hat at the farmer's retreating wagon.

Seamus turned about on his buckboard seat and waved back. "Sure'n you're welcome!"

Marty watched his forefather until Seamus was out of shouting range. Lucky for Marty, Seamus's generosity had won out over Maggie's practicality, and he'd gotten a ride to the railroad tracks. Instead of having fourteen miles to go, now he only had six. Six miles wouldn't be that bad, would it?

Marty looked down the tracks, a set of red iron bars that looked like they met on the horizon—a horizon that didn't show any sign of the town of Hill Valley. He realized there was only one way to find out how long six miles could be.

Marty started to walk down the railroad tracks.

• • •

Maybe he misunderstood Seamus, and he was going the wrong way. Surely he had walked six miles by now. It felt like he'd walked twelve!

Marty squinted. Was there something up ahead? He'd seen hallucinations before—pools of water that weren't really there, trees and houses that turned out to be rocks and boulders. Marty walked a little faster. This was the first hallucination that had a hanging sign—a sign that read HILL VALLEY.

Marty started jogging. That was no hallucination. The sign was real. It was the Hill Valley train station!

It wasn't much to look at, though. As he got closer, Marty realized the depot was even smaller than his great-great-grandfather's farmhouse. Marty guessed that made sense. Hill Valley had only been founded a few years before. It would still be a pretty small town.

And a pretty quiet town, too. There wasn't much activity at the train depot. A Chinese fellow in what looked like black pajamas was sweeping the platform. Another fellow was standing in front of a window marked TELEGRAPH OFFICE, and at the far end of the platform, a farmer was pulling boxes and bales of hay from his wagon. Well, what was Marty expecting? Gunfights? A brass band welcoming committee? This was the *real* old west after all, not some movie starring John Wayne or Clint Eastwood—no matter what he'd called himself back at the McFly farm.

He walked past the farmer's wagon and saw

that he was on the road that led into the town of Hill Valley.

Marty stopped and whistled. Hill Valley really looked like something out of the wild west, even, sort of, like a western movie. A dirt road led down the main street, past an old barn on the left, and a row of stores on the right, fronted by a raised, wooden sidewalk.

Marty passed by a corral, fronted by a large sign:

HONEST JOE STATLER
FINE HORSES SOLD—BOUGHT—TRADED

These were the same Statlers Doc had told him about—the ones in the new and used-car business in 1985. Marty guessed some things didn't change.

Marty looked at the row of stores to his right, a saloon, a barbershop, a general store, the Hill Valley newspaper office, a Chinese laundry, a post office—and there were men riding horses, folks in wagons, even a fellow walking along with a shovel and cart (the sign on the side said A. JONES. MANURE HAULING.)—everything you'd expect in a real western town.

People were looking at him kind of strangely as he passed. Marty wondered if it was his hat. Or, he worried again, could Doc really have been wrong about his fancy shirt and pants? Wouldn't a scientist know about that sort of thing?

Marty looked up at a banner stretched above the street.

HILL VALLEY FESTIVAL—SATURDAY
NIGHT, SEPTEMBER 5
Dance—Food—Games
Proceeds to Construct the Clock Tower.

Wow. They were just building the clock tower now. This place had a real sense of history.

He stopped when he saw he was opposite the Marshal's Office. The place looked like it was closed up tight. There was even a sign on the front door:

"The marshal has gone to Haysville to witness the hanging of Stinky Lomax."

He stopped again. There, directly in front of him, was the town square, or what would become the town square. The courthouse was only halfway built. The marble pillars were there, but scaffolding covered most of the building, and there was a large, round hole in the tower where the clock was going to go.

In front of the courthouse-to-be was a flagpole, complete with a somewhat different-looking American flag. There wasn't much wind today. Marty made a quick count—there were only thirty-eight stars.

The square was bordered on two sides by hitching posts. A few of the posts had teams of horses and wagons tied there. Beyond them Marty saw a brick building that housed a Wells Fargo Office, and, farther down the street, the Essex Theater—also under construction—and, roped off from the street, the remains of a burned-out building. Hill

Valley looked like a small town that was growing pretty fast. Marty bet something was about to get built in that burned-out lot as well.

There was one more building on the street, the grandest of them all, a full two stories high. It looked brand-new, with a brightly painted sign: PALACE SALOON & HOTEL.

The place looked like the real center of town. Marty guessed that if he was looking for information, this Palace was as good a place as any to start.

Marty heard the sound of galloping horses. He turned around to see a stagecoach leave the Wells Fargo office—a stagecoach headed straight for him!

Marty jumped out of the way. Shouldn't stagecoach drivers look where they were going?

Ugh. He wrinkled his nose. Something really stank around here. He looked down at the ground, and the horse manure he had walked into.

Gross. When would he learn you had to be careful when you were traveling in time? Probably never. Heck, his carelessness when he had been in 1955 had almost gotten himself—well, not killed, but almost not born, which was pretty much the same thing. He couldn't let that sort of stuff happen here. He had to watch his every step.

But, in the meantime, he had to get this manure off his sneaker. He looked around for a likely place and decided he would wipe it off on the edge of the wooden sidewalk. That done, he entered the saloon through the swinging doors.

It looked like a wild west saloon on the inside,

too—a real big wild west saloon. There was a long bar at the far end of the room, complete with a couple of cowboys, bolting back shots of whiskey. There was a balcony that ran around three sides of the main room. Women in low-cut, frilly dresses leaned against the polished wooden railings. In the old western movies, Marty remembered, they always called these women "saloon girls." They glanced at Marty as he walked into the room. Mostly, though, they looked bored.

The rest of the main room was filled with round, wooden tables. A couple of them had groups of men around them, playing cards. And, wow. Marty stared at the silver vase at the end of the bar. Was that an honest-to-goodness spittoon?

Three of the cardplayers—older fellows with well-worn clothes who kept their drinks and pistols on the table and looked like they might all have come out of old western movies themselves—glanced up as Marty walked past.

"Take a look at what just drifted in the door," cackled the first of the three, a clean-shaven, heavy-set fellow wearing a vest and brown derby hat.

The second fellow, who sported a tall, black hat and snow-white beard, took the cigar out of his mouth to add: "Why, I didn't know the circus was in town."

"He musta got that shirt off a dead Chinee," added the third fellow from behind his drooping, dark mustache. All three men at the table laughed.

"My son once come home from back east wearin' fancy ass duds like that," the oldster with the derby drawled.

"What'd you do?" the fellow with the beard asked.

"I set fire to him," the first one allowed.

Gee, Marty thought. Maybe his clothes *were* a little out of place. They were probably a little too new, for one thing. And, Marty guessed from what he saw other people wearing as he wandered through town, maybe they weren't used to the pearl buttons, fringe, and fancy stitching in this part of California. But he didn't have time to worry about clothes and things like that now. He could think about that stuff after he'd found Doc.

He walked up to the bar. The bartender stared at him for a long moment. Marty wondered if maybe his clothes were *really* out of place.

"What'll it be, stranger?" the bartender asked at last.

What'll it be? Marty was supposed to order a drink? He hadn't thought this far ahead. Still, this was a bar and all. He didn't want to seem too out of place. He wanted to get some information out of these people, after all. He guessed he should order something. But what? He was almost positive they didn't have Diet Pepsi in the old west.
· "Uh, well, I'll have—" Marty began. Tab and Diet Coke seemed out of the question, too. "—uh, some ice water?"

The three old-timers burst out laughing behind him.

The bartender, however, wasn't amused. He

shook his head and pointed at the door. "You want water, you can use the horse trough outside there." He reached beneath the bar and picked up a brown bottle and a shot glass. "In here we sell whiskey."

The barkeep plunked the glass on the table and poured Marty a drink. A bit of the whiskey splashed on the top of the bar. The spot where it hit the wood started to smoke.

Marty stared at the smoking bar top. "Actually," he confessed, "I'm just looking for the blacksmith."

Somebody yelled loudly behind him:

"Hey, McFly!"

Marty turned around. A mean-looking fellow dressed all in black—complete with black hair, black stubble, a long, black, handlebar mustache, and a scowl that would encourage anybody to walk in the other direction—pushed his way through the swinging doors. He was followed by three other guys who didn't look much nicer—in fact, all three of them looked like finalists in a mean-and-stupid contest.

"McFly," the man in black demanded as he approached Marty, "I thought I done told you never to come in—"

He stopped and stared at the somewhat overdressed teenager.

"Hey," he said, his voice no friendlier than before, "you ain't Seamus McFly. You look like him though, especially with that dog-ugly hat. Are you kin to that hay barber? What's your name, dude?"

"Uh—" What should he say? Marty decided he

might as well stick with the same story he'd used with Seamus and Maggie. "Eastwood. Clint Eastwood."

"Clint Eastwood?" the man in black jeered. "What kind of stupid name is that?"

"Hoo-ee!" said another of the newcomers, this one with even more stubble than his boss. "I'd say he's the runt of the litter!"

The second of the sidekicks puffed on his cigar as he stepped forward to peer into Marty's mouth. "Hey," he yelled to the others from around his cigar, "lookee at these pearly whites! I ain't never seen teeth this straight what warn't store bought."

The third sidekick, whose long face made him look—if that were possible—even dumber than the others, pointed at Marty's feet. "And take a gander at them moccasins. What kinda skins is them? And what's that writin' mean?"

The guy with the cigar frowned down at Marty's sneakers. " 'Nee-Kay.' Must be some kind of Injun lingo."

The man with the black mustache slammed a fist down on the bar. "Bartender! I'm lookin' for that no-good, cheatin' blacksmith. You seen 'im?"

The bartender took a step back. "Uh, no, sir, Mr. Tannen."

"Tannen?" Marty asked. He took a step toward the leader of the gang. "*You're* Mad Dog Tannen!" Now that he looked at the guy, he did look something like his great-grandson, Biff.

Tannen looked back at Marty, his expression as grim as Biff in his worst possible mood.

" 'Mad Dog'?" he demanded, almost choking on the words. "Nobody calls me Mad Dog! I hate that name! I hate it, you hear!"

Whoops, Marty thought. Now who was the stupid one around here? He had just made another mistake without even trying. Marty stepped back toward the bar and lifted his arms from his sides, to show he wasn't carrying a gun. Would Mad Dog Tannen shoot an unarmed man? Probably, Marty realized. After all, in a few days, he was going to shoot Doc Brown in the back.

"This oughta prove interestin'," one of the old-timers cackled as all three put down their cards. Marty had the feeling that every eye in the saloon was looking at him.

Marty hoped it didn't get *too* interesting. It wouldn't help Doc much if Marty ended up getting killed first.

Mad Dog stared down at Marty. "The name's Buford Tannen. *Mister* Buford Tannen. I don't hold with no disrespect, especially not from no duded-up, egg-suckin' gutter trash!" Mr. Buford Tannen drew his revolver. "Dude!" Tannen paused just long enough to let a smile curl up the corner of his mouth. "Let's see how good them fancy ass shoes are for dancin'."

He pointed his gun at Marty's sneaker.

"Dance!"

He fired. The bullet left a hole in the floor inches away from Marty's toes!

Tannen aimed at Marty's other foot. He pulled the trigger again.

Marty hopped sideways as the bullet hit the floor.

Mr. Buford "Mad Dog" Tannen laughed. "That's right, *dance!*"

Tannen's three sidekicks pulled their guns and started to shoot, too. Marty hopped from foot to foot. Maybe, he thought, he should have taken that gun from Doc after all. Except, Marty realized, if he had been packing a gun and was playing by Mad Dog Tannen's rules, he would probably be dead by now.

"C'mon, runt," Tannen demanded, "you can dance better than that!" He aimed the muzzle of his revolver even closer to Marty's toes.

Marty hopped faster. Buford and his bad guys hooted and cheered.

This wasn't going to work. Marty had to do something besides hopping, or sooner or later, one of those bullets was going to hit one of his feet. He had to get out of here somehow. He needed some kind of diversion.

Maybe, Marty thought, if he changed his style of dancing—

Marty stopped hopping and started to moonwalk.

"Billy Jean is not my lover—" he whispered as he moved. Hey, he hadn't watched all those Michael Jackson videos for nothing! And it worked, at least for a minute. These cowboys had never seen somebody walk backward on his toes. They had stopped shooting, and were watching him, openmouthed.

But Marty knew the shock value of his dance

couldn't last forever. He needed a bigger, noisier diversion. He looked quickly to either side, looking for something—a chair, maybe, or a beer glass—anything he could toss to make a noise and get out of here. But the bar behind him was empty, and everything else in the saloon was on the other side of Buford and his boys, completely out of reach, unless Marty felt like getting shot. But there had to be something! Tannen cocked his pistol. He seemed to be getting bored with the moonwalk. Marty knew, as soon as Mad Dog started shooting again, his sidekicks would join in. Marty looked down at his soon-to-be-hopping feet.

Wait a minute! There was a warped floorboard near his sneakers, a plank that had popped out of the floor near the end of the bar. And, resting on the other end of that plank was the spittoon.

Perfect! Marty moonwalked quickly to the warped board. If he could stomp on that plank just right, maybe he could get that spittoon to jump into the air and crash somewhere, getting everybody to turn their attention someplace else, and giving him a chance to get the heck out of here.

He twirled around, jumped, and whooped—the last mostly for dramatic effect—landing with all his weight on the warped plank.

And the spittoon went sailing, way up into the air, way farther than Marty ever thought it would. Maybe, Marty considered, this wasn't quite the diversion he was looking for. He realized the silver vase was headed straight for Mad Dog Tannen.

There was a loud clang as the spittoon hit Tannen in the head, knocking him down and spraying him with spit and old tobacco.

The saloon became very quiet. The three sidekicks stared down at their boss, who sat there, stunned, dripping tobacco juice.

Tannen blinked. His mouth turned down into what started as a frown but quickly turned into a look of intense rage as he wiped the brown sludge from his face with the back of his hand.

The old-timer with the white beard whistled softly at Marty. "You'd better run, boy. Fast. And far."

Marty looked at the beet-red Buford, the three sidekicks with guns still drawn, and the saloon door, only a few steps away. The old-timer, Marty realized, was quite correct.

"Right," Marty replied. He hopped up on the bar, then leapt for the chandelier. His momentum carried him right over Buford and the boys as he swung across the room. He let go of the chandelier and landed right in front of the swinging doors.

"Five dollars says he doesn't live more'n five minutes," he heard the oldster with the derby drawl.

"Ten dollars says he don't last four," the codger with the mustache replied.

But Marty wasn't turning around, because he also heard the boots of Tannen and his gang as they clomped after him.

Marty ran through the swinging doors and jumped from the sidewalk. Horse manure or no horse manure, he ran down the middle of the street. He glanced over his shoulder and saw Mad Dog's three sidekicks run from the saloon, followed by Tannen himself. Well, Marty had gotten away from Tannen's gangs before, in other places and other times. He had a good head start, too. With any luck, he could get far enough ahead of them to find a place to hide.

He risked another look behind. The three sidekicks were getting on their horses.

Marty ran even faster.

He heard the sound of hooves galloping in the dirt, followed by whoops and raucous laughter.

So much for outrunning them. Maybe he could dodge them, though, or run through a store or a narrow alleyway where horses couldn't follow.

He glanced back again. All four cowboys were bearing down on him—and Buford Tannen was twirling a lasso! They didn't even have to catch up to Marty! They could toss a rope over him and pull him in!

Marty was having trouble catching his breath. He had run too far, too fast—just after he had hiked six miles into town. He needed something that was faster than a horse—something like that pink hoverboard—twenty miles away, stuck back in the DeLorean outside that bear cave.

He looked back in the direction his feet were going, and almost ran into a man on a horse. Marty stopped as the horse reared. He didn't want to fall under those hooves!

A lasso fell around his shoulders. Buford and his boys had caught up with him! Marty tried to tug it off, but the rope was yanked tight, pinning his arms to his chest.

All the commotion out in the street had brought some of the local townspeople out of the stores along the street to watch. But none of them interfered. Marty imagined all the townspeople already knew about Mad Dog Tannen's temper, and what lengths he would go to when he was riled, not to mention covered with gunk from a spittoon—something that Marty, unfortunately, was going to learn firsthand.

Tannen turned his horse around and pulled Marty, half walking, half stumbling, back up toward the saloon.

"We got us a new courthouse!" Tannen called to the others with a grin. "High time we had a hangin'!"

Meanwhile, back in the Palace Saloon:

The bartender squinted out a dirty windowpane. Mad Dog Tannen had followed his boys out into the street, and was laughing with the others as they dragged the helpless dandy between their horses. And the marshal wouldn't be back from the Stinky Lomax hanging for a couple of hours yet. There was only one thing to do.

The barkeep waved for Joey to come close, then whispered in the youngster's ear:

"Better get the blacksmith."

•Chapter Eight•

Mad Dog Tannen tied his rope to another one, looped through a pulley that hung from a section of the courthouse scaffolding. Some of the towns-people gathered around to watch, but all from a safe distance from Tannen and his gang. With the marshal out of town, Marty guessed, no one was going to step in and save him. It was all too much like those westerns he used to watch on TV; *High Noon* or something. Except for one thing; in those movies, the good guy Gary Cooper or John Wayne or Clint Eastwood or somebody, stepped in at the last minute to save the day. Now that he was in the real old west, the good guy was about to get hung.

But now that they'd stopped, maybe Marty could get out of this mess. He tugged at the rope, lifting it above his shoulders.

The rope was jerked from his hands as Tannen tightened it around Marty's neck! It was too tight. He was choking.

The bad guys had Marty down. But they had left his hands untied. He grabbed at the rope, trying to breathe, but the noose wouldn't come loose. There was no way to struggle, no way to escape. Marty wondered if his life would flash before his eyes in those last few seconds before he died. That was supposed to happen, wasn't it? Marty wasn't so sure, though—the last few days alone had been so confusing, what with all the time-traveling and everything, he didn't think it could all flash by in a few seconds.

Buford had tied the other end of the pulley rope around his saddle horn. He backed his horse down the street, and the rope tightened over the pulley, closing around Marty's neck and dragging him to his feet. Maybe Marty was worrying for nothing. He wasn't going to have time for any kind of flashbacks. He grabbed the rope above his Adam's apple, jerked it loose enough to take another breath.

Tannen and his cronies were all laughing, as if this was the funniest thing they had ever seen. Marty wondered if this was all some sort of big practical joke with them, until he twisted around to look in Mad Dog Tannen's eyes. There was anger in there, and more than anger, like those eyes might have been a little crazy, too.

Tannen backed up his horse again, and Marty was lifted in the air for a second before his feet hit the ground again. No, Tannen and his boys were still going to kill him. They just wanted to play around with him a little first.

Marty heard a gunshot. A brick shattered on a corner of a building—a brick close to Mad Dog Tannen's head.

The sound of the gun had come from in front of Marty, across the street. Marty saw a man with a rifle standing in the door to the local blacksmith's shop.

"Cut him down, Tannen," the man demanded.

Even before he heard the voice, even with the brown duster coat and the tall, black hat Marty recognized that man in the doorway.

"Doc!" Marty called.

The rope jerked up again, lifting him from the ground.

"Well, well," Tannen remarked casually, as if he and Doc had just met at a Sunday picnic, "if it ain't the blacksmith. Just the man I come in to town to see." He rested his hand indifferently on his holstered gun. "We got us some business to settle."

Marty kicked out, trying to touch the dusty street with his toes. But he was too high off the ground now. The rope was too tight around his neck. He couldn't pull it free. He couldn't breathe.

"The only thing we got to settle," Doc called back, "is that you cut him down and get outta here."

"I don't see where you're in any position to be tellin' me anythin'," Tannen replied. He glanced at his henchmen with a wide grin. "Boys—"

All three sidekicks whipped out their revolvers.

"Three guns against one," Buford pointed out. "And I haven't even drawn yet. The odds ain't exactly in your favor, smithy."

Doc raised his rifle in reply. With the additional height the noose around his neck gave him, Marty could see everything quite clearly, maybe too clearly. Doc's rifle looked like a Winchester, except it had some sort of special addition. The inventor had rigged up some kind of telescope on top of it, not some little sight, but a full-size telescope tied to the top of the rifle. Marty blinked— Doc and the rifle were going out of focus. His vision was starting to blur. He had to breathe, or he wasn't going to be looking at anything—ever again.

Doc fired.

And Marty hit the ground. Doc's bullet had cut right through the rope! Marty grabbed the noose and pulled it away from his neck.

"It'll shoot the fleas off a dog at five hundred yards, Tannen," Doc called as he reaimed his Winchester, "and it's pointed straight at your brain, so I'd say the odds are *definitely* not in your favor."

Tannen glared at Doc for a moment, then grinned amiably, waving for his boys to reholster their guns, while he dismounted.

"You owe me money, blacksmith," Buford remarked as casually as before.

Doc lowered his gun, but kept his finger resting near the trigger.

"How do you figger?" Doc asked.

"My horse threw a shoe," Buford explained, still grinning, "and seein' as you was the one who done the shoein', I say that makes you responsible."

Doc shook his head in disbelief. "Well, since you never paid me for the job, I say that makes us even."

"Wrong!" Buford's face fell into a much more natural scowl. "See, I was on my horse when he threw the shoe, and I got throwed off. And you know what happened when I got throwed off? I busted a perfectly good bottle of fine Kentucky Red Eye." His hands turned into fists as he thought about it. "And that made me so mad that I shot that damned horse and then I had to go off and git me a new one!"

Tannen paused and grinned back at Doc. "Now, the greaser I stole him from said that horse was worth seventy-five dollars. So, the way I figger it, blacksmith, you owe me seventy-five dollars for one horse and five dollars for the whiskey." He opened both his hands, then rested the right one lightly on the handle of his gun. "I'll take cash money now, or you can pay with your life later."

Oh, no! Marty realized. That's what the tombstone meant!

"That's the eighty dollars—" he mumbled aloud.

"Look," Doc said reasonably, "if your horse threw a shoe, bring him in and I'll reshoe him."

But Doc's suggestion threw Mad Dog Tannen back into a rage.

"What's wrong," he demanded. "Are you deaf? I told you, I done shot him!"

But Doc wasn't going to get tripped up by Buford's logic.

"That's your problem, Tannen," he replied.

"Wrong!" Buford roared. "It's yours! So from now on you better look behind you when you walk, 'cause one day you're going to get a bullet in your back. And in the two seconds it takes for you to hit the ground, you'll remember that it was me that done it."

Doc still wasn't impressed. "That doesn't sound very Christian to me, Tannen."

But Buford grinned at that. "It's in the good book, smithy. An eye for an eye! One blacksmith for one horse!" He glanced at the three members of his gang. All three nodded back, agreeing with Tannen's logic.

Tannen tugged his horse's reins as if he was going to turn away, but his other hand whipped his gun from its holster.

Doc had the rifle pointed straight between Tannen's eyes.

"Try it, Tannen," Doc suggested.

Buford snickered and let his revolver fall back in its holster. He looked at his henchmen and spoke to them in a low voice: "Saturday, boys."

Tannen dug his spurs into the flanks of his mount and led his gang—shooting, whooping, and hollering—down the street and out of sight.

Marty stood up, massaging his neck. He was glad that he'd found Doc at last, and that he was still alive. Now all they had to do was get out of here!

Great Scott!

Doc walked quickly over to his teenage friend—the last person he ever expected to see in 1885.

"Marty," he announced sharply, "I gave you explicit instructions not to come back here, but to go directly back to 1985!"

Marty gave up rubbing the rope burns on his neck to smile at the inventor. "I know, Doc."

That was it? He knew? Doc could think of all sorts of reasons why Marty shouldn't be here. But, then again, now that he thought of it, hadn't he helped Marty get here, back in 1955? Of course he had—he had clear memories of sending the teenager and the DeLorean off not once, but twice. That was pretty important, wasn't it? Why hadn't he remembered that before?

Oh, of course. He hadn't remembered it, because, until Marty had shown up in 1885, he hadn't helped Marty get back to 1885. In other words, Marty, by coming here, had not only changed the past—that is 1885—but he had changed Doc's past in 1955 as well. It was another one of those time travel paradoxes, probably the first of many, now that both he and Marty were back in the old west.

Why, the implications of their confrontation with Mad Dog Tannen alone—what, for example, if they had killed Mad Dog Tannen back there, and then, because he was dead, Buford never got around to fathering a child, and, because his grandfather was never born, there would no longer be any Biff Tannen, and, since there was no Biff, Marty and Doc wouldn't have to go into the past because of that sports almanac, and, when they didn't go into the past, the DeLorean would no longer be struck by lightning, therefore not sending it back to—it was too confusing. Doc decided not to think about it for the moment.

"But it's good to see you, Marty," he said instead. And he meant it. As fascinating as the old west was, he didn't realize how much he missed his own time and friends until he saw the teenager's face out there, about to be hung in front of the courthouse. But now it was time for more practical matters. Doc examined his friend critically.

"Marty," he said as gently as possible, "we've gotta do something about those clothes. You walk around town dressed like that, you're liable to get shot."

Marty rubbed his neck again.

"Or hanged," the teenager agreed.

Doc shook his head. "What idiot picked out that outfit?"

Marty grinned sheepishly. "You did, Doc."

Oh. Now that he thought of it, he had, just before he'd sent Marty back here from 1955. Doc even remembered his reasoning: Roy Rogers dressed like this, didn't he? It was real western hero stuff. Unfortunately, all of Doc's research into this matter had been conducted when he was a teenager sitting in Saturday matinees.

He apologized quickly to the teen and suggested they go someplace a little less public. Marty needed to change his clothes, and Doc decided he would prefer somewhere that his back wasn't such an open target to Buford and his boys. He would have to be doubly careful now that he'd managed to get on Mad Dog Tannen's bad side.

Doc led Marty back to his blacksmith's stable, remembering, rather wistfully, when he thought the old west would have been a good place to find some peace and quiet.

As soon as they were inside, Marty gave Doc the photo of the tombstone. Now that he'd met Mad Dog Tannen, he really knew they had no time to lose.

Doc Brown, in turn, gave Marty a pile of old clothes, real old western work clothes, to choose a new outfit from. Doc had set up his shop in that old, dilapidated stable that Marty had passed when he first came into town. It was typical that Doc hadn't thought to put a sign outside to advertise his services. Still, Marty guessed, in a western town as small as Hill Valley, word of a new blacksmith probably got around pretty fast.

Doc had fixed the inside of this place up pretty well. He'd divided the stable up into three different parts. There were living quarters at one end, a stable with a handful of horses at the other, and, in between, all the blacksmith stuff, including a forge and anvil, plus some of Doc's usual inventions, improving on the local tools. Marty read the horses' names on the stable doors as he pulled on jeans, a workshirt, a pair of boots that actually fit, and a sarapé, just like the real Clint Eastwood always wore in those spaghetti westerns. GALILEO, the first horse's sign read, then ARCHIMEDES, and NEWTON. He grinned. No matter when Marty ran into him, you could always depend on Doc for some things.

Doc, for his part, stared at the photograph of his tombstone for a long, long time.

" 'Shot in the back by Buford Tannen, over a matter of eighty dollars'?" he said at last, reading the gravestone's inscription on the snapshot. "September seventh, 1885—that's this Monday!" He glanced up at the calendar behind him—trust Doc to have a calendar—the square kind with each page with a single date. Today's page read "Thursday, September 3."

Only four days, Marty thought.

"Now I wish I'd paid him off," Doc muttered. "And who's this 'beloved Clara'? I don't know anyone named Clara."

"It sounds like she's"—Marty didn't know how to tell Doc this—"like she's a girl friend or something?"

That, at last, got Doc to look up from the photograph. "Marty," he lectured, "my involvement in such a social relationship here in 1885 could result in a disruption of the space-time continuum. As a scientist, I could never take that risk, certainly not after what we've been through!"

"Emmett!" a voice called from outside. "Ho, Emmett!"

Doc stopped his pontification as a man wearing

a suit and derby hat stepped through the stable door.

"It's the mayor!" Doc called back to Marty. He turned to the newcomer. "Hello, Hubert."

"Excuse me, Emmett," the important-looking newcomer apologized jovially. "Remember at the town meeting last week you volunteered to meet the new schoolteacher at the station when she came in? Well, we just got word she's coming in tomorrow. Thanks for helpin' us out, and here're the details for you."

He handed Doc a piece of paper, quickly speaking again before the other man had a chance to reply: "Oh, and her name's Miss Clayton. Miss Clara Clayton."

Doc's mouth dropped open as the mayor turned around and quickly left the stable.

"Well," Marty remarked softly to end the silence, "now we know who Clara is."

Doc shook his head, still not taking his eyes off the paper the mayor had given him.

"Marty, it's impossible. The idea that I could fall in love at first sight—it's romantic nonsense! There's no scientific rationale for that concept."

Marty grinned at that. They had finally come to a subject where Marty was the expert.

"Doc," he said gently, "it's not a science. When you meet the right girl, it just hits you, like lightning."

Doc looked up, all color drained from his face. "Marty, please, don't say that."

Oh, that's right, Marty thought. Doc hadn't had the best experiences with lightning. Maybe though, if Marty tried to explain things a little better, Doc would see this could be a good thing.

Doc walked over to a large machine and switched on what appeared to be a steam-powered motor. Wheels spun, gears turned, and a long conveyor belt jerked forward as smoke spurted from the top. What was Doc doing? Well, whatever it was, Marty was still going to make his point.

"When I first met Jennifer," he started again, "we couldn't take our eyes off each other. We just—clicked." He stopped for a second and thought about the woman of his dreams; the way her pale face was framed by dark brown hair, the way she smiled when she saw Marty, the way she kissed. And he had left her in a war zone that he had created when he'd let Biff steal that sports almanac!

"Jennifer! I sure hope she's all right. We just left her on her porch swing—"

Now it was Doc's turn to be reassuring. "She'll be fine, Marty. When you burned the almanac in 1955, the normal time line was restored. That means that once we're back in 1985, you just have to go over to her house and wake her up."

Marty really hoped that was true. This time travel business could sure get confusing. "Once we're back in 1985," Doc had said. Boy, did Marty want to get back there now!

The machine began to clang violently. What was Doc doing?

"Marty, quick!" Doc barked, pointing at the lower left corner of the wildly vibrating device. "Turn that valve all the way to the left!"

Marty did as he was told. The machine coughed, and a single ice cube dropped onto the table below. Doc dropped the cube into a glass and filled it with brown liquid from a kettle.

"Iced tea?" he offered Marty.

Marty shook his head. "No thanks."

Doc glanced at the paper one more time. "I guess Miss Clayton will have to find other transportation." He shoved the paper in the pocket of his overalls. "Let's go get the DeLorean and get ourselves back to the future."

Oh. Maybe, Marty thought, he should have told the inventor about this before.

"Uh," he began rather hesitantly, "well, there's one minor problem, Doc. I ruptured the gas tank when I landed. We'll have to patch it and refill the tank."

"Great Scott!" Doc Brown exclaimed, clapping a hand to his forehead. "You mean you're out of gas?"

"Yeah," Marty replied with a sinking feeling. Doc was even more upset than Marty had expected.

"What, is that some kind of big deal?" Marty was confused. Hadn't Doc made improvements to the DeLorean when he was in the future? "We've still got Mr. Fusion."

"Mr. Fusion powers the time circuits and the flux capacitor," Doc explained patiently. "But the internal combustion engine runs on ordinary gasoline. It always has." He slammed a fist into his other hand. "There isn't going to be a gas station around here until sometime in the next century!

And, without gasoline, we can't get the DeLorean up to eighty-eight miles per hour!''

Oh, no! When Marty cracked the gas tank running away from the Indians, had he stranded both of them in 1885?

If so, Marty realized, Doc might be just as good as dead.

•Chapter Nine•

Now this was traveling, western style!

Doc and Marty had ridden out to the hidden DeLorean with half a dozen horses from Doc's stable. It had only taken them a couple hours to get there on horseback—although by the end of their hard ride, Marty's saddle had felt a little too solid under his rear end. Perhaps, he thought, he should ease into this horseriding a bit more gradually.

For a change, though, luck was with them when they reached the car. The bear wasn't in its cave—or even in the immediate neighborhood—and they hooked up the team of horses to the front of the DeLorean in only a few minutes. Now, with the sun setting slowly in the west, they were driving the car almost like a stage-coach across the open prairie, Doc holding the reins, and Marty—glad to be off the horse—riding shotgun. Except, instead of holding a gun, Marty was holding the car's digital speedometer.

Doc urged the horses on as Marty called out their speed:

"Seventeen—twenty—twenty-two—twenty-four!" Come on horses, he thought. Go, go, go! "Twenty-two—twenty-three—twenty-two—" He looked up. Couldn't the team gallop any faster?

Doc read Marty's expression and shook his head.

"It's no use, Marty," he said with a shrug. "Even the fastest horse in the world won't run faster than thirty-five or forty miles per hour."

Yeah, Marty thought, he could see why Doc had objected to this experiment in the first place. But there were only six horses pulling them now. What if they got a bigger team—a much bigger team?

"But," he pointed out to Doc, "since it's a 130 horsepower engine, couldn't we just hitch up 130 horses?"

Doc only shook his head. "Even if we could, it just doesn't work that way."

Yeah. Now that Marty thought about it, it didn't make sense to him either. Horses just couldn't gallop at eighty-eight miles an hour.

That meant, once they got back to Hill Valley, they had to come up with something else—and something fast. More than anything else, it had to be fast.

* * *

It had been well after midnight by the time Doc and Marty drove into town. The streets were dark and empty, they had thrown a drop cloth over the top of the car, and Doc had even devised these special covers for the tires that looked like wagon wheels, all to make the DeLorean look more like a wagon—a particularly lumpy wagon, maybe, but a wagon nonetheless.

Doc drove the team and the DeLorean right into his barn, and, after closing the door against any possibility of prying eyes, announced that they should both get a good night's sleep. They had to be alert in the morning to continue their experiments. Good old Doc. Marty should never have doubted him for a moment. If there was a fast idea to be had, the inventor would have it.

With morning, Doc brought out four lanterns and placed one by each corner of the car so that they could see their way around the DeLorean, even in the barn's dim interior. Marty got the privilege of crawling under the car to get a look at the damage. The puncture in the gas tank wasn't very big at all, maybe half the size of a dime, just big enough to let all the gasoline drain out.

Doc surmised that the empty tank had been dried out by the desert heat, so there'd be no fumes or residual gasoline to get in the way of repairs. Using his blacksmith's forge and some scrap metal, Doc had the tank patched in only a few minutes more. Marty was impressed by how proficient Doc had become with the smithy's tools.

While they let Doc's handiwork cool, the inventor pulled out a bottle of whiskey. Marty thought about saying something, about this not being the best time for a drink and all, when Doc opened the hood of the car and poured the whole bottle into the gas tank. Doc told Marty to get behind the wheel.

"The bartender said this is 180 proof," Doc explained as he shook the last drops from the bottle. "If this works, we're home free." He took a step away and nodded to the teenager. "Try it, Marty."

Marty turned the key in the ignition. The engine whined, but then it turned over! Marty cheered and Doc whooped. The DeLorean would run on alcohol!

There was a tremendous explosion at the back of the car, like somebody had fired a gun. Marty cut the ignition as Doc ran back to investigate.

"Damn!" Doc yelled as he pulled up the rear hood. "It blew the fuel injection manifold!" He looked at the bottle still in his hand. "That hooch peddlar must put more in his stuff than just whiskey!" He frowned as he peered in at the smoking wreckage. "It'll take a month to rebuild it!"

"A month?" Marty despaired. "Doc, we haven't got a month!" He climbed back out of the car. "You're gonna get shot on Monday!"

Doc tossed the empty whiskey bottle in a rain barrel by the door. He sighed and looked at Marty.

"I know—" He paused, hitting his forehead

with the heel of his hand. "Wait—I've got it! We can simply roll it down a steep hill!" He paused again, and began to pace. "No—we'd never find a smooth enough surface—unless—of course! Ice! We wait until winter, when the lake freezes over!"

"Winter?" Marty asked incredulously. The inventor was getting deeper into science, leaving reality farther and farther behind. "What are you talking about, Doc?" He walked over to the wall and pointed out September 7 on the calendar. "Monday is three days from now!"

"Damn!" Doc slammed his right fist into his left hand. "All right, let's think this through logically. We know it won't run under its own power, and we know we can't pull it. But if we could figure out a way to *push* it up to eighty-eight miles an hour somehow—"

Doc's voice trailed off. How, Marty thought, could they possibly push it that fast?

They both stood there for a moment in hopeless silence.

Then, in the distance, a train whistle blew.

Great Scott!

Their luck was holding, if you could call it luck. They had heard the whistle blow, and looked out the back window of the barn to see the train pull into the station. The train was sitting at the Hill Valley depot by the time they got there, and would be there for a few minutes still, while they unloaded the clock face for the top of the courthouse tower. It was an ideal opportunity for them to quiz the engineer.

Doc let Marty do most of the talking. The teenager was good at that sort of thing—much more so than Doc, who did better with dogs and machines—and Marty got the engineer talking right away.

"How fast can she go? Why, I've had her up to fifty-five myself." The grizzled train man patted the chugging locomotive by his side. "They say that fearless Frank Fargo got one of these up to near seventy out past Verde Junction."

Marty nodded eagerly, acting impressed, which pleased the engineer no end.

"Is it possible to get it up to ninety?" Marty asked.

The engineer frowned at that. Doc wondered if even Marty was being too obvious.

"Ninety?" The engineer whistled. "Tarnation, son, who'd ever need to be in such a hurry?"

Maybe it was time for Doc to pitch in.

"It's a bet that he and I have, that's all," he added reassuringly. "Theoretically speaking, *could* it be done?"

The engineer chewed on his tobacco a moment before he replied.

"Well, I suppose if you had a straight stretch of track with a level grade"—he scratched his head—"and you warn't haulin' no cars behind you"—he paused to spit—"and if you could get the fire hot enough, and—" He took another chaw, then offered it to Marty and Doc. They both politely refused. "—and I'm talkin' hotter than the blazes of hell and damnation itself, mind you, then"—he considered it another second, then nodded—"yessir, it might be possible to get her up that fast."

He and Marty glanced at each other. This was better news than Doc could have hoped for!

Doc turned back to the engineer. "Tell me, when's the next train come through here?"

The engineer spat before he considered the question.

"Monday morning at eight o'clock," he said at last.

Marty and Doc looked at each other again. Monday morning was cutting it awfully close, but it would have to do.

The workmen yelled down that they'd gotten the clock face loaded on their wagon. The engineer called back to them as he climbed back into the cab to start the train. Doc glanced down at the huge clock disk on top of the buckboard at the other end of the train platform. The huge circle was bordered by the numbers one to twelve, but the clock face itself didn't have any hands— at least not yet. He got the oddest sensation from the sight, as if, for that clock, at least, time hadn't yet begun. Doc wished, for a change, that he could stop time himself. It was probably because, if they couldn't get the DeLorean to go fast enough, time could quite possibly be stopping him.

He waved for Marty to follow him into the train station. It was time to get to work. There, on the wall of the waiting room, was the map of the train system for the whole Hill Valley area.

He led Marty over to the map. "If we can find a long stretch of level track that will still exist in 1985, we can push the DeLorean with the locomotive!" He quickly studied the terrain the train would cover after leaving Hill Valley.

"Here!" he exclaimed, pointing out the spot on the map to Marty. "This spur that runs off the main line three miles out to Clayton Ravine—" He paused, frowning at the map. "Funny, this map calls it Shonash Ravine. That must be the old Indian name for it, before they changed it."

He grinned back at Marty. It looked like the teenager still didn't quite understand. "It's perfect. A nice long run that goes clear over the ravine—you know, over near that new Hilldale housing development."

"Yeah, right," Marty answered, finally remembering the spot Doc described. But it was the teenager's turn to point at the map. "Doc, according to this, there is no bridge."

Great Scott! Doc thought.

Time travel was never easy.

The map back at the station had been a little confusing. They had to go out and take a look at the actual site. Which meant riding horses again.

Marty remembered, not so long ago, in 1955, when he had asked Doc if he might get a chance to ride a horse. Now, he almost wished he had never seen a horse in the first place. Marty—who had just finished a twenty-mile ride out to rescue the DeLorean the day before—was back on a horse again. He hoped—someday—his rear end would forgive him.

In the meantime, though, they reached the bridge—or, at least, what there was of it. Just like half the town of Hill Valley, the bridge was still being built. Only half the trestle had been finished, with a set of tracks that stopped midair, a hundred feet over the ravine below.

There was a big sign on the edge of the ravine:

SHONASH RAVINE BRIDGE
SCHEDULED COMPLETION, SUMMER 1886.
CENTRAL PACIFIC RAILROAD

It looked just like all those highway construction signs when his family went on long trips—except that it didn't say anything about your tax dollars at work. Marty wondered if they had tax dollars in the old west.

He shook his head. It didn't matter what kind of dollars they had out here. The only thing that mattered was that this bridge wasn't built.

"Scratch this one," he said to Doc. "We sure can't wait around a year and a half for this thing to be finished."

But Doc only grinned back at Marty.

"Marty, it's perfect," Doc insisted. "You're just not thinking fourth-dimensionally."

"Huh?" Marty didn't get it.

"As you said," Doc explained, "the bridge will exist in 1985. It's safe and still in use. Therefore, as long as we can get the DeLorean up to eighty-eight miles an hour before we hit the edge of the ravine, we'll instantaneously arrive at a point in time where the bridge is completed. We'll have track under us and coast safely across the ravine."

But, Marty thought, to get the DeLorean up to that sort of speed, they needed to be pushed by something—like a train engine.

"What about the locomotive?" he asked.

"It'll be a spectacular wreck," Doc conceded. "Too bad no one'll be around to see it."

They were going to wreck a locomotive?

Marty was about to ask another question—something about paradoxes and Doc always talking about their responsibility to the past—when he heard the woman scream.

"Great Scott!" Doc yelled.

There, coming right at them through a cloud of dust, were two runaway horses pulling a woman on a buckboard. Somehow, the woman had lost the reins, and now wasn't able to do much more than cling onto the wagon for dear life.

And it looked like horses and wagon were heading straight for the ravine!

•Chapter Ten•

Great Scott!

Doc Brown spurred his horse to intercept the runaway wagon. At great risk to her own life, the frightened woman had somehow managed to reach forward and grab the reins from where they had fallen atop the wooden beam that harnessed the team to the wagon. She was a plucky female, Doc had to give her that!

But he was gaining on the careening buckboard! The horses pulling the wagon were galloping wildly, jerking the wagon back and forth in a zigzag line, while Doc's trusty horse, Archimedes, was heading straight and true to intercept the buggy before it reached the precipice. In mere seconds, Doc and his stead had drawn parallel to the rear of the buckboard—close enough to see the trunk and traveling bags leap with every rut and protrusion the wagon wheels encountered.

The woman yanked hard on the reins. The horses turned in response, but the wagon was traveling too fast! The sudden change in momentum caused the team's yoke to snap, and horse and wagon parted company. The horses had turned, and were galloping to safety, but the wagon was still headed straight for the edge!

C'mon, Archimedes! Doc thought. The horse sprang ahead until Doc was right alongside the front of the buckboard. Doc reached down and wrapped his arm around the woman's back, lifting her from the speeding wagon and onto the horse before him.

The buckboard hit a large rock, turning over and dumping its contents on the ground before it flipped over a second time, falling over the edge into the ravine.

As Doc pulled Archimedes to a halt, he could hear the crash of the wagon as it smashed into splinters far below!

He dismounted, then helped the woman off his horse. Doc remembered to breathe. He had seen that rescue move over and over again on Saturday afternoons, in any number of Roy Rogers and Tim Holt westerns. Still, he was glad it actually worked in real life.

He took his first real look at the woman he had saved.

"Thank you, sir," she began as she turned her face to look up at him.

And what a face. Doc stopped breathing all over

again. Her face had been hidden in shadow before, framed by that attractive bonnet. But then she smiled.

And what a smile. Doc thought it was like looking at the sun for the first time.

"You saved my—" She paused as she, too, really looked at Doc.

She sighed the sweetest sigh Doc had ever heard. "—life," she concluded.

And what wonderful features surrounded that smile! That pert nose, that strong chin, those deep, large brown eyes that a man could get lost in—Doc sighed, then realized that, perhaps, he should say something in turn.

"You're quite welcome, Miss—?" Doc asked, surprised, in a way, at his forwardness.

"Clayton," she answered readily, her smile still firmly in place. Ah, Doc thought. If only he could bottle that smile and keep it next to his heart. He had never met a woman like this in his entire life—not in 1985, or even 2015! But he should introduce himself as well.

"Emmett Brown, at your service."

She curtsied slightly. What a gentlewoman she was—and here in the old west! Her every word was a symphony, her every move worthy of a sonnet.

"Pleased to meet you, Mr. Brown," she answered in a voice Doc liked better with every word she uttered. "Very pleased, indeed."

"The pleasure is all mine, Miss Clayton," Doc replied very sincerely. "But please, call me Emmett."

"In that case, Emmett," she responded demurely, "please call me Clara."

Yes, Doc thought. Clara. An old-fashioned name, but sweetly old-fashioned; a perfect fit for a perfect woman. And the way she had said his name, Emmett—the word had never sounded so good before.

"Clara," he repeated, seeing what her name sounded like on his tongue. "What a beautiful name. Clara."

"Clara?" a voice asked behind Doc. Whoever could that be?

Oh, that's right. He remembered now. Marty was here, too. What, with the excitement of the rescue and all, Doc had forgotten just about everything.

Clara, he thought again, as he looked at the woman, who looked back at him.

" 'Beloved Clara'?" Marty asked behind him.

Doc glanced behind him. What was the teenager going on about now? And what was Marty doing, staring at that photograph?

Marty was worried. He had never seen Doc act like this—ever!

First off, Doc seemed to have forgotten all about their need to get out of here, or the fact that he was going to get shot at the end of the weekend. In fact, Doc seemed to have forgotten about anything besides Clara Clayton. Where the woman was concerned, Doc was the most efficient Marty had ever seen him. The inventor had retrieved the team of horses, and, with Marty's aid and the use of some spare petticoats, strapped the woman's trunk and suitcases between the team. Then, with Clara seated behind him, he had smartly led all of them to Clara's new home. But when Marty had tried to bring up the business with Mad Dog Tannen—in fact, when Marty had tried to even interrupt Doc and Clara's conversation—he hadn't gotten anywhere at all.

Doc led the party to a small wooden house surrounded by a white picket fence. He dismounted and gallantly turned to help Miss Clayton from the horse.

"This is your house," he said, his eyes never leaving Miss Clayton's face. "It comes with the job. The schoolhouse is just down the road." He looked away from her at last to nod at the teenager.

"Clint, let's help Miss Clayton with her bags."

"Please," Miss Clayton objected with a smile, "that's not necessary. I can take care of them. You've done more than enough already."

Doc looked back to the woman in his life. "But it's really no trouble—"

Marty realized it was time to step in, before the two of them went on like this until Doc got shot on Monday. Wow. His old friend was really hooked on this lady. Marty hoped he never acted this loopy with Jennifer.

"Doc," Marty interjected gently, "she says it's fine, and we've gotta get going." He nodded to the woman. "Miss Clayton, it was nice to meet you, good luck with your schoolteaching and all."

Doc finally started to walk toward his horse.

At last! Marty thought.

The inventor turned back to the schoolteacher.
"Oh, Clara," he began as his gaze locked once again with hers, "I'll straighten out everything with Mr. Statler for the buckboard rental, don't you worry about that." He paused awkwardly before continuing. "I feel somewhat responsible for what happened."

Miss Clayton nodded her head. "Why, that's very gentlemanly of you, Mr. Brown—Emmett." She paused, and when she spoke again, there was a certain wistfulness in her voice. "You know, I'm almost glad that rattlesnake spooked the horses. Otherwise, we might never have met. I suppose it was"—it was her turn to pause—"destiny."

She held out her hand. Doc took it. They stared at each other.

"Thank you," Clara said after a moment. "For everything."

"You're quite welcome," Doc replied eventually.

Miss Clayton frowned slightly. "I will see you again, won't I, Emmett?"

Marty shook his head no. They had things to do before Doc got shot!

But Doc wasn't looking at Marty. "Of course," he replied. "You'll see lots of me, I'm sure. I have a shop in town. I'm the local scientist—uh—and blacksmith."

Miss Clayton broke back into her smile. "Science? What sort of science? Astronomy? Chemistry?"

Doc blushed a bit. "Actually, I'm a student of all the sciences."

Marty almost groaned. This was too much. These two were going to grin themselves to death.

Marty couldn't be polite anymore. "Doc, we gotta get going."

His voice seemed to break the spell. Doc glanced at him a little guiltily before he turned back to the schoolteacher.

"Yes, well, excuse us, Clara, we have to get going." He raised a hand to wave. "Toodle-loo."

He took a step back, bumping into the picket fence.

Miss Clayton almost giggled. "*Hasta luego*, Emmett," she said instead. She turned and sighed.

And Doc *finally* got on his horse.

Marty had lost all patience with this. As soon as they were out of hearing distance of Miss Clayton's place, he turned his horse to stare at his old friend.

"Doc!" was all he said.

But Doc knew what he meant. "Well, I might see her again, just in passing," the inventor explained apologetically. "And I didn't want to hurt her feelings. After all, she did have quite a scare. Miss Clayton almost ended up at the bottom of Clayton Ravine"—Doc stopped suddenly, his eyebrows raised in surprise—"*Clayton Ravine?*"

Marty realized what Doc meant. It was so obvious. Why hadn't he seen it before?

"Holy shit, Doc," he explained, his words chilling him as he recalled his history class. "Clayton

Ravine was named after a schoolteacher who fell over the cliff there about a hundred years ago—" He stopped. It felt like his heart was encased in ice. "I mean, this year!"

Doc stopped his horse dead.

"Great Scott, Marty! Are you sure?"

Marty nodded grimly. "Positive. Every kid at school knows that story because we've all had teachers we wish would fall into that ravine." Or truancy officers, Marty added silently. He couldn't remember the number of times he wished Mr. Strickland could have found his way to the bottom of that ravine.

All the color had drained from Doc's face. "Then she was *supposed* to go over in that wagon and"—he had to force himself to go on—"and die. And now, I've altered history."

Doc gasped. "This is heavy." He frowned, his brow furrowed in concentration. "I guess that means we'll have to take her back there and push her off—"

Doc stopped, openmouthed. "What am I saying? We can't do that!" He ran a hand through his frizzy hair. "I don't know what to do! Damn, I wish I had never invented that infernal time machine! It's caused nothing but disaster!"

Marty had never seen his old friend this upset.

"Doc, it's not a disaster," he said softly. "I mean, what's the worst that can happen? They don't name the ravine after her. It's no big deal. Everything will be fine."

Doc sighed. "I hope you're right."

Marty hoped so, too. He remembered what had

happened when Biff had changed the future and turned 1985 into a place slightly worse than the black hole of Calcutta.

Marty hoped more than anything that if they could get back to 1985, it would be the 1985 they remembered.

•Chapter Eleven•

Saturday, September 5, 1885

Doc had shaken Marty awake at first light, and after another of the inventor's hearty breakfasts, they had set to work with everything they had from the present blacksmith shop, and the future DeLorean. They only had two days; they had to work fast.

Marty spoke into the circa-1985 walkie-talkie he'd brought along in the DeLorean: "Testing, testing, one two—great, Doc, they still work!"

Doc smiled tautly. "All right, Marty, let me show you the entire plan and layout." He waved for Marty to follow him over to the far side of the barn. There, on a weathered, rough-hewn table, was another of Doc's famous homemade tabletop models, full of wooden blocks, toys, scrap metal, and anything else Doc could scavenge from 1885. Marty realized the model was supposed to be the town and immediate surroundings of Hill Valley 1885. Marty glanced over at his friend. He had noticed that Doc looked a little haggard. While Marty had slept, the inventor must have been busy on this table.

Doc's fingers ran along a miniature version of the train tracks as they left town. His hand stopped, and his index finger pointed to a location some distance outside of Hill Valley.

"Tomorrow night, Sunday," he explained, "we'll load the DeLorean onto the tracks here, on the spur." His finger moved on to a point where the track split in two. "This switch track is where the spur goes off the main line and out to Clayton"—Doc stopped to clear his throat—"Shonash Ravine."

He glanced up at Marty to make sure the teenager was following. Marty nodded. Now that Doc pointed out these places, Marty realized they had ridden by them the day before.

Doc pointed back at the edge of town. "The train leaves the station at eight Monday morning. We'll stop it here." He indicated a spot just before the train reached the spur to the ravine. "Then we'll uncouple the cars from the tender, throw the switch track, and then we'll hijack"—Doc cleared his throat again—"borrow the locomotive and use it to push the time machine."

He looked back up to Marty. "You'll get in the DeLorean, while I open up the locomotive throttle and put her into a full highball. Then I'll climb across and into the DeLorean. According to my calculations, we'll reach eighty-eight miles per hour just before we hit the ravine"—Doc pointed at where the track ended abruptly on the edge of the tabletop model—"at which point we'll be instantaneously transported back to 1985 and"—his finger drew a line from where the track ended, out across empty space—"we'll coast safely across the completed bridge."

But Marty had spotted something he didn't understand. "What's the red X on the windmill for?" he asked.

"That's our fail-safe point," Doc explained. "The point of no return. Up until there, we still have enough time to stop the locomotive before it plunges into the ravine. But once we pass that windmill, it's the future or bust."

Doc turned on his large steam generator, the same one he'd used the day before to make ice cubes. The huge machine chugged to life, wheels spinning, gears turning, belts whirring, as Doc attached a couple of cables from the machine to the train tracks.

"Watch!" he called, glancing up at Marty. "I would have used flashlight batteries, but they haven't been invented yet."

The model locomotive started up as Doc completed the connection, pushing a roughly carved wooden model of the DeLorean. The model train chugged right along, gaining speed as it approached the edge of the table. At the last possible second, Doc snatched the DeLorean, as the model locomotive fell off the edge and onto a pillow Doc had left on the floor.

Doc grinned broadly. "It couldn't be simpler!"

Somebody knocked on the door to the barn.

"Emmett?" a woman's voice called.

The door opened to reveal Miss Clayton, holding a telescope.

"Clara!" Doc called.

Uh-oh, Marty thought. They didn't have time for the schoolteacher to start asking embarrassing questions. He grabbed a horse blanket from the door to a nearby stall and quickly covered the DeLorean.

"Why, hello," Doc continued as Clara stepped into the barn. "This is quite a surprise!"

Miss Clayton smiled a bit sheepishly. "I hope I'm not disturbing you—"

"Who, me?" Doc interrupted perhaps a bit too quickly. "No, no. I was, uh, just conducting a little experiment here."

He took a step toward the schoolteacher. "So, uh, are you getting settled?"

She smiled, not particularly bothered that Doc had changed the subject. "Yes, I'm starting to get settled." She looked down at the long black object in her hands. "Emmett, when my bags were thrown from the wagon, my telescope was damaged and, well, since you mentioned an interest in science, I thought you might be able to repair it for me." She stepped closer to Doc in turn.

"I'd pay you, of course," she added hastily.

"Oh, no," Doc said as he accepted the telescope from her outstretched hands. "I wouldn't think of charging you for this." He paused as their hands brushed ever so briefly. He cleared his throat.

"Let me have a look—" He extended the telescope and lifted it to his eye.

"I think a lens may be out of alignment," Miss Clayton explained, "because if you move it like this"—she stepped next to him as she turned one of the telescope tubes—"the image turns fuzzy. See? But if you turn it this way—"

She stood on tiptoe so that her head was right next to Doc's as she twisted the telescope again. Doc turned to look straight into her eyes.

"—everything becomes clear," he finished hoarsely.

Oh, no, Marty thought. The two of them were going loopy again. Marty couldn't believe this. Look at both of them, staring into each other's eyes like that. Marty wouldn't get involved in this sort of thing, and he was only a teenager, for goodness's sake! Well, come to think of it, there was that one time when Jennifer and he had been at archery practice together . . .

The other two were still staring. It was Marty's turn to clear his throat.

Doc and Miss Clayton both quickly looked away. Doc examined the telescope with great interest.

"It's a very simple repair," he remarked, not looking at the schoolteacher.

"Then I'll just come back for it in a few days," Miss Clayton replied, avoiding Doc's eyes as well.

"Oh, I can repair it this evening and have it for you tonight—" Doc's voice trailed off as he looked at her again.

This had gone too far. It was time for Marty to stop the whole thing.

"Tonight?" he interrupted. "Doc, we were gonna check out that festival deal tonight, remember?"

The inventor continued to smile at the schoolteacher. How could Marty get Doc to remember they had to get the DeLorean ready for time traveling without mentioning it? Oh, yeah.

"For the clock tower?" Marty added.

"Oh," Doc replied, vaguely, his smile falling to the slightest of smiles, "right—"

"Why, yes, the town festival," Clara said brightly. "I planned on attending that myself." She smiled at Doc as she stepped away from the telescope. "Well, in that case, I'll see you tonight at the festival, Emmett." She walked quickly toward the door, turning once more before she left. "And thank you for taking care of my telescope."

She waved as she left the barn. Doc sighed and turned to look at the telescope as if it were the most wonderful thing he had ever seen.

Marty sighed, too. The inventor had definitely gone loopy. Marty had the feeling he wasn't going to be able to talk Doc out of this one, either. He just hoped that a little trip to the town festival didn't lead to a bullet in Doc's back.

Now that they were here, Marty had to admit it. This festival was something else again. And as long as Doc insisted they needed the break, Marty might as well try and enjoy all this.

The whole of the main street was lit by bright

red Chinese lanterns, with American and California State flags hanging from the big saloon and the unfinished courthouse. Carnival booths had been set up in the street. The first one was called EL SAPO—it looked like you were supposed to toss wooden discs into the open mouth of a large clay frog. Farther down the line was an arm-wrestling booth, occupied at the moment by a huge ox of a guy, sitting patiently at a table; a photographer with a sign announcing HAVE YOUR PICTURES TAKEN WITH THE NEW CLOCK TOWER! and another booth advertising RECORD YOUR OWN VOICE! with a primitive phonograph machine that recorded onto cylinders that looked like they were made of wax. Beyond them were tables full of food and drink; fried chicken and steaks, lemonade and cider.

But first, Doc and Marty had to pass a table with a very large sign: PLEASE CHECK ALL FIREARMS. The table was piled high with revolvers and a half-dozen rifles, with a couple of deputies hovering behind to make sure the sign was obeyed. Marty and Doc both paused at the table long enough to assure the deputies they were unarmed, then went in to join the festivities.

There were hundreds of people on the streets, far more than Marty had thought lived anywhere around Hill Valley. Some wandered past the carnival and refreshment booths, and a few hung around near the bandstand, but by far the greatest group was gathered near the courthouse, where a wagon held the new clock face, now attached to a huge clockwork mechanism and festooned with bright red ribbons.

That well-dressed fellow who had come by the barn climbed up on the clockwork wagon. Marty and Doc must be just in time for the big ceremony.

The well-dressed guy doffed his derby hat and raised his hands for all the townspeople to quiet down. When they finally did, he started to speak:

"As Mayor of Hill Valley, it gives me great pleasure to dedicate this clock to the people of Hill County. May it stand for all time."

He pulled a lever, which released a catch on a large gear on the clock mechanism. With the ribbon no longer holding it, the gear began to spin.

The clock ticked from 8:00 to 8:01.

The crowd cheered. The brass band began to play "The Battle Hymn of the Republic."

Doc nudged his friend's shoulder. "You know, Marty, in a way, it's fitting that you and I are here to witness this."

Doc was right. They were there when the clock was struck by lightning and finally stopped running, and now here they were, at the beginning.

"Yeah," he agreed. "Too bad I didn't bring my camera."

Marty and Doc looked at each other.

It only took Marty a minute to bring over the photographer.

"The only problem is," Doc muttered as they both posed by the new clock, "we'll never be able to show it to anybody."

Apparently, Marty realized, Doc had forgotten this picture showed up in the history book. Should he remind him? After all, the picture had already been there in 1955. Still, Marty realized, now that future picture would show both Doc and Marty. Maybe, he thought, Doc had enough to worry about already.

"Smile, Doc" was all Marty said.

The photographer ducked under the curtain behind the box camera. The flash powder ignited. For an instant, the night turned blinding white.

Marty blinked, trying to get his eyes used to the Chinese lanterns again. He turned to say something to Doc, but Doc was gone. Marty ignored the white spots in front of his eyes, and searched the crowd, until he spotted his inventor friend, walking rapidly toward a smiling Miss Clayton.

Marty sighed. He guessed it was up to him to pay the photographer.

Great Scott!

Clara was coming, wasn't she? She said she would be here. Doc thought she wanted to see him. What if she had had second thoughts? Doc looked through all the people around the bandstand, where a group of musicians were about to begin a square dance. So many people! He really wished the crowd wasn't quite so large. She could be here already, and the two of them could miss each other in the mob. They should have come up with a more specific place to meet. And maybe, Doc thought, he should have worn something fancier than a clean shirt and a bolo tie. Waiting for a woman could certainly be a nervewracking experience. Doc Brown sighed. With due apology to Marty, Doc felt like some sort of foolish teenager.

Then the crowd parted, and Clara was there. She was wearing a ruffled, red calico dress that shown in the Chinese lantern light. She looked even prettier than Doc remembered.

He walked toward her, and she turned and saw him. Their gazes locked the way they had the day before, and Doc swore he felt an electrical charge in the middle of his chest. Extraordinary, he thought.

Doc offered his arm as he reached her side. "May I have this dance, Miss Clayton?"

She draped her arm around his. "I would be honored, Mr. Brown."

And with that, the fiddles, banjo, and piano started a song on the bandstand, while a fellow with a guitar called the steps.

There were certain things that science just didn't teach you. A case in point, Doc Brown realized, was square dancing.

Clara was very patient as the dance progressed, and for that Doc was very grateful. It was simply that so much of this was new to him. Why, until this dance began, he wouldn't have even been able to recognize a "dosey-doe!" And to be quite frank, he still wasn't sure of the exact nature of an "allamand left." But he could do nothing but give his all, especially where a lovely woman like Clara was concerned.

"Swing your partner!" the caller yelled over the bouncy tune.

That sounded easy enough. Doc and Clara

grabbed each other's hands and spun around. Clara was laughing. Lord, he loved to hear that woman laugh. He wouldn't mind spending the rest of his life listening to that woman, and looking at her smile.

That was, if he could keep from tripping over his feet.

Great Scott!

Marty didn't know quite what to do with himself. Doc and Clara were busy dancing, and while Doc didn't seem to always know exactly where his feet should go, the two of them looked like they were having a really good time.

"The Doc in love," he murmured to himself. "Who woulda thought?"

Marty wished he felt that happy. Even though he was surrounded with people whooping and hollering, eating and drinking, dancing and singing, Marty was feeling sad and empty. Actually, he realized maybe it was because of all these happy people here, not one was the person he really wanted to see. Watching Doc and Clara laughing and dancing and carrying on—Marty sighed. He wished Jennifer were here, it was that simple. Or, perhaps, he *really* wished he were back in 1985 with Jennifer, and that everything were back the way it had been before all this time machine business. But that couldn't happen until Monday—if it could happen at all.

Well, being depressed wasn't going to help him get back to the future. Maybe if he walked by the carnival booths, he could snap out of it. Marty wandered over to a booth at the far end of the line; one he hadn't looked at yet. Actually, it was a wagon, with an elaborate sign painted on the side:

ELMER H. JOHNSON
PURVEYOR OF THE WORLD'S FINEST
SHOOTING INSTRUMENTS!

Marty walked around to the other side of the wagon and joined the crowd. The other side of the wagon was open, and inside was an impressively elaborate shooting gallery, with metal bears peaking from behind boulders, ducks on revolving wheels, and mechanical gunfighters and Indians marching along on a belt-driven line.

A man in a bright checkered suit and derby hat stood before and a little to one side of the wagon, calling to the crowd—a fellow, Marty guessed, whose name was Elmer H. Johnson.

"Step right up, gentlemen," Johnson suggested, waving at a table covered with shining new pistols, "and test your mettle with these latest products of Colonel Sam Colt's Patent Fire Arms Manufacturing Company of Hartford, Connecticut, U.S.A."

Marty realized this guy was a salesman, and this place was a lot closer to an auto showroom than a carnival shooting gallery. These guns were all here for demonstration and sale.

Johnson picked up one of the pistols. "Take this one for example—the new improved and refined Colt Peacemaker—yours for a mere twelve dollars." He laughed insincerely. "I tell you true, the action on this new model is smoother than the finest whiskey in President Cleveland's liquor cabinet." He paused to take a deep breath, as if he could smell the whiskey. "And how smooth is that? Why, it's so smooth that even a baby could handle this model, and that's a fact."

The salesman looked straight at Marty.

"How about you, young fella?" He waved the pistol, handle out, in Marty's direction. "Why don't you give it a try?"

Me? Marty thought. Fire a gun? He shook his head.

"Uh, no thanks," he replied politely. "I'm not too experienced with those—"

But Elmer H. Johnson wasn't going to take no for an answer. "Son," he continued evenly, his insincere smile still firmly in place, "I said that even a baby could handle this weapon. Surely, you're not afraid to try something that even a baby could do?"

How did Marty get himself into these things? Still, he didn't like what this salesman was implying.

"No," he insisted, "I'm not afraid, I just don't—"

"Well, then," the salesman insisted, offering the gun one more time, "step up here like a man."

Like a man? Marty bristled. This guy was implying that Marty wasn't a man? That was almost as bad as being called chicken!

Marty took a step forward.

"All right," he said, holding out his hand. "Sure."

The grinning salesman handed him the pistol.

Wow! This thing was heavy. Still, if he got the right kind of grip on the pistol he should be able to manage it. He took the gun in both hands and aimed at the wheel of ducks. He fired.

The gun jumped in his hand. The bullet hit the side of the wagon.

Some of the crowd laughed.

So they were going to laugh, huh? They thought he was chicken, huh? Marty would show them!

He just had to get the hang of this thing. Maybe if he pretended to draw the gun from a holster— that was the way cowboys always did it in the movies.

He gripped the gun as he looked back at the wheel of ducks. Now he had to pull it out in one fluid motion, aim and point.

The gun fired almost before he could think about it.

The duck was down!

Hey! All right, Marty thought. Clint Eastwood couldn't have done any better.

And nobody laughed this time around.

Marty decided to try again. He aimed and took out a bear, and then an Indian.

"Not bad, son," the salesman admitted.

"Yeah," Marty agreed, "it's just like video-games." Especially that one game he always used to play, Wild Gunman.

Johnson grinned at him as he reloaded the pistol. "Let's speed it up a little bit."

Yeah, Marty thought, just like Wild Gunman. Now, all he had to do was use the pistol like the plastic gun on the videogame.

He shot six times. Three ducks, two gunfighters, and a bear went down beneath his bullets.

The crowd applauded. Mr. Johnson shook his head.

"Just tell me one thing, fella," the salesman asked. "Where'd you learn to shoot like that?"

Marty shrugged as he put down the empty pistol.

"Seven-eleven," he replied.

Johnson turned to the crowd as Marty walked away.

"That kid's a natural if I ever saw one."

All right, Marty thought. He was feeling better already.

But Marty wouldn't have felt so good if he could see Buford and his boys stride up to the edge of the festival.

"You sure the blacksmith's gonna be at this here shindig?" one of the gang asked nervously.

Buford Tannen laughed, a genuinely ugly sound.

"Sure he's here. Everybody's here tonight."

Buford didn't sound nervous in the least.

He knew just what he was here for.

•Chapter
Twelve•

You could always depend on Buford Tannen, if you were looking for something underhanded.

The deputy stepped forward, blocking Tannen and his gang from entering the town square.

"You gentlemen are gonna have to check your firearms," the deputy said firmly, "if you want to join in the festivities."

But Buford Tannen only smiled as his gun hand reached casually for his belt.

"And who's gonna make us, tenderfoot?" Tannen drawled. "You?"

"I am," Marshal Strickland remarked as he clicked back the hammer on his shotgun. He urged his horse out of the shadows, and his ten-year-old son stepped out with him. Strickland had hoped to have a few quiet minutes to talk to his son—that was, until Buford Tannen showed up.

Buford was the sort of character you had to deal with directly.

"Why, Marshal Strickland," Tannen said smoothly as he turned to face the lawman. "I didn't know you were back in town."

Strickland stepped forward. "If you can't read the sign, Tannen, I presume you can read *this*."

He pushed the barrel of the sawed-off shotgun against Tannen's spine.

"You're a pretty tough hombre when you're shovin' a scattergun in a man's back," the outlaw remarked.

"I'm like you, Tannen," Strickland replied grimly. "I take every advantage I can get. Now are you gonna check your iron?"

Tannen only grinned. "Hey, I was just joking around with your deputy. Of course I'm gonna check my iron." He unbuckled his gunbelt. "We all were, weren't we, boys?"

The three gang members all agreed as they un-strapped their gunbelts and tossed them on the table.

"Smile, Marshal," Tannen drawled as he added his gun to the others. "After all, this *is* a party."

Strickland pulled his shotgun back, but kept it aimed at Tannen.

"The only party I'll be smiling at," he replied, "is the one that sees you at the end of a rope."

Buford laughed at that, then waved for his boys to follow him into the festival.

Strickland looked down at his boy. "That's how you handle 'em, son. Don't give an inch, and maintain discipline at all times. Remember that word, son—*discipline*."

His son nodded solemnly. He was a good boy, and he would learn the Strickland Code.

Discipline. Now, the marshal thought, all he had to do was keep an eye on Buford Tannen.

After all that shooting, Marty deserved a little grub. He checked out all the food tables and decided a piece of blueberry pie would fit the bill nicely.

"Why, Mr. Eastwood!" a man's voice called. Marty looked around to see the whole McFly family, Seamus, Maggie, and baby William.

"It's nice to see you again," Seamus said heartily. "I see you got yourself some respectable clothes, lad. And a fine hat."

"Yeah," he explained a bit sheepishly, "the one you gave me, well, it wasn't my style."

"Sure'n that one suits you, Mr. Eastwood," Maggie added generously. "Very becoming."

"Thanks," Marty replied, grateful for his great-great-grandmother's politeness.

Marty glanced back at the piece of pie in his hand, and saw something he could barely believed stamped in the pie tin that had come along with it—the words FRISBIE PIE COMPANY.

He showed the tin to both Seamus and Maggie. "Hey, check this—Frisbie! That's far out!" He grinned. He'd never thought about it, but he guessed Frisbees had to come from someplace.

Seamus and Maggie, though, seemed to be a little confused by Marty's demonstration.

Seamus turned to Maggie. "Far out?"

Maggie shrugged at her husband. "It's right there in front of him."

Old west, Marty told himself. You have to remember you're in the old west.

He consoled himself with a bite of pie.

But Marty wouldn't have been so hungry if he had been watching the dance floor.

The band was playing "My Darling Clementine" as Tannen and his boys walked up. They surveyed the couples waltzing around the street corner that served as the dance floor.

"There he is, Buford." The sidekick with a cigar pointed to the middle of the mass of dancers. "Dancin' with the piece of calico."

Tannen grinned as he saw the blacksmith dancing close with the woman, and got that glint in his eye that his boys knew. It was time for mischief.

"What you gonna do, boss?" another of his men asked, doing his best to match Tannen's sneer.

Their boss lifted his hat and pulled out a tiny gun—a single-shot derringer. He looked at the members of his gang.

"I figure if I bury this muzzle deep in his back"—Tannen chuckled—"nobody'll hear the shot."

"Careful, Buford," the last gang member cautioned. "You ain't got but one shot with that."

But Tannen only grinned. "I only need one."

He hid the derringer in his meaty hand and

walked toward Doc and Clara. The rest of his gang followed at a respectful distance.

Doc could dance like this forever. Waltzing with the woman of his dreams to the sweet sound of a fiddle, breathing in the fragrance of her hair, he had never felt so alive at any time in his life—indeed, in any of the many different times he'd managed to live through.

He felt a sharp pain in his back, like something hard was jabbed against his ribs.

"I told you to watch your back, smithy," a gruff voice said behind him.

What? That sounded like Mad Dog Tannen. But it couldn't be! He wasn't supposed to be killed for a couple days!

Doc stopped dancing.

"Tannen?" he called, trying to keep the fear out of his voice. "What are you doing here? It's not Monday yet!"

"I come to kill you, smithy," Tannen replied.

The hard thing jabbed into Doc's back again.

"It's a derringer," Tannen explained. "Small, but effective. Last time I used it, fella took two whole days to die—bled to death inside." He chuckled. "It was real, real painful. That means you'd be dead about suppertime on Monday."

Suppertime on Monday? Two days to die? But Doc wasn't ready—especially now that he had found Clara. He had been too smug, confident he could escape this villain with the use of the time machine. But now he realized that he died on

Monday didn't mean he had to be shot on Monday.

Doc could feel the sweat run down his forehead. Tannen had his derringer pressed right against Doc's innards. The minute Doc tried to escape, or make any kind of move against him, Tannen would simply pull the trigger. And Doc, in this day before wonder drugs and modern surgery, would slowly bleed to death.

Emmett Brown took a ragged breath. Wasn't there something somebody could do? Or was he already a dead man?

•Chapter Thirteen•

Clara stepped forward. The nerve of this bearded fellow!

"Excuse me," she said boldly. "I don't know who you think you are, but we're dancing."

The dark-bearded fellow smiled at that. Now that she got a little closer to him, she noticed that he could stand a bath.

"Well, lookee what we have here!" he called to the lady, then turned back to Emmett. "Aren't you gonna introduce me to the lady? I'd like to dance."

But her escort shook his head firmly. "I wouldn't give you the pleasure." Emmett stood up straight and defiant. "You'll just have to go ahead and shoot."

"Well, now's as good a time as any—" the bearded fellow agreed all too quickly.

Wasn't this like a couple of men—stubborn to the end. Well, as sweet as Emmett was, Clara didn't need a man to defend her honor.

"No, Emmett," she interrupted firmly. "I'll dance with him. I'm not going to allow you to be shot for my sake."

She turned to the newcomer. And as for this smiling low-life, did he still think he was out on the frontier or something? Maybe somebody had to show him that Hill Valley had become a civilized town.

"Your dance, Mr.—?" she began.

"Tannen," he obliged. Well, at least he had that much courtesy.

He turned to three gentlemen who appeared to have come with him. "Boys, keep the blacksmith company while I get acquainted with the filly." He pushed Emmett over to the waiting arms of all three. They grabbed him, preventing him from coming to her aid.

The more Clara saw of this Mr. Tannen, the less she liked him. She might be new to the West, but the place and time didn't matter. She could always recognize a bully.

The man in black waved her over, his smile even bigger than before. She noticed he still held that tiny pistol in his hand; the same pistol he had threatened Emmett with.

"Mr. Tannen," she said sternly, "I don't dance very well when my partner has a gun in his hand."

"You'll learn," Tannen replied. He grabbed her and started to dance, but now he held the gun at her back. She could feel the sharp metal edge of the muzzle through her dress.

Well, gun or no gun, she supposed she had promised to dance with him, so she should at least go through the motions. It was the sort of thing a proper woman did, no matter what the circumstances.

Mr. Tannen pulled her closer.

"You know, smithy," he called over to Emmett, "maybe I'll just take my eighty dollars' worth out of her."

"Dammit," Emmett yelled back, straining against the three sets of arms that held him. "Leave her out of this, Tannen."

"Yeah," Mr. Tannen said as he turned to her again. "I figure there's something you can do that's worth eighty dollars."

So dancing wasn't going to end this? Clara supposed she had been naive to think it would be that simple. Still, she'd be a pretty poor school-teacher if she didn't have a few ways to deal with bullies.

"Eighty dollars?" she replied sweetly. "Why, Mr. Tannen, I believe you've underestimated me."

The smile returned to Mr. Tannen's not-too-bright face. The bully thought he had won.

"Have I now?" he asked in triumph.

Clara could feel the pressure of the gun leave her back. This, then, was the perfect time.

She stomped down on his foot with her patent leather shoe, then kicked him sharply in the shin.

"Owww!" Tannen screamed, grabbing for his

foot. He glared at Clara, then pushed her roughly away. She lost her balance and fell to the ground.

"Stop it!" she could hear Doc yell. "Leave her alone!"

And then the music stopped.

Marty was famished. He finished off the pie in a matter of seconds. That was one of the problems with time travel—it never left you time to eat.

The square dance music ended in the middle of a song.

"Damn you, Tannen!" he heard Doc yell.

Uh-oh, Marty thought. While he was eating pie, Doc was getting into trouble. He saw people moving quickly off the dance floor. It looked like there was going to be a fight. Marty decided he'd better get over there before things got serious.

"No," he heard Buford Tannen reply. "I damn you—to hell!"

The crowd backed away even more, so that Marty could see Mad Dog Tannen had a derringer in his hand—a derringer that he had pointed straight at Doc!

Things had gotten serious already, too serious for Marty to get over there and do anything before Tannen pulled the trigger. But he couldn't just stand here and do nothing!

Marty looked down at the pie plate still in his hands. He whipped it at Tannen with his best Frisbee toss. And the plate sailed straight and true, right into Tannen's gun hand!

The gun went off. Buford's gang backed off as the bullet sailed through Doc's hat.

Tannen turned to look at Marty.

"You!" he yelled.

Marty saw Doc break away from Buford's gang and run to Clara, helping her up from the ground. It looked like the worst was over.

"Just leave my friends alone," Marty replied.

But Tannen didn't want to leave it at that. "Them's mighty strong words, runt," he called. "You man enough to back 'em up with more than a pie plate?"

Marty didn't have time to argue with Buford Tannen, especially if they had to get out of here by eight o'clock on Monday morning. He turned and started to walk away.

"What's wrong, dude?" Tannen called after him. "You yellow?"

Marty paused. *Yellow?* No, he told himself, he didn't have time for people to call him names, either. He and Doc had a date to get out of here.

"That's what I thought!" Tannen exclaimed with a laugh. "A yellow belly!"

A yellow belly? That was worse than being called chicken!

Marty turned back to the sneering Tannen. "Nobody calls me yellow!"

"Then let's finish it," Mad Dog declared. "Right now."

One of Tannen's boys tugged on his boss's sleeve.

"Not now, Buford," the gang member murmured. "The marshal's got our guns."

Tannen blinked and looked at his sidekick, then glared back at Marty.

"Like I said," Tannen called, "we'll finish it—tomorrow."

Another of his gang members nudged him. "Tomorrow we're robbing the Pine City Stage."

Buford turned and looked at his boys. "What about Monday? We doin' anything on Monday?"

The three gang members looked at each other.

"No," said the first sidekick—the one that had tugged on Tannen's sleeve, "Monday's fine. You can kill him on Monday."

Tannen turned back to Marty, the smile once again on his face. "I'll be back this way on Monday. We'll finish it then, right over there"—he pointed beyond Marty—"in front of the Palace Saloon."

Marty didn't believe all this was happening. "Yeah, right," he replied skeptically. "When? High noon?"

"Noon?" Tannen laughed derisively. "I do my killin' before breakfast. Seven o'clock!"

Killing? Before breakfast? Marty suddenly realized that—as stupid as Mad Dog Tannen might be—this was for real. He could get himself killed before he got a chance to get back to the future.

Marty swallowed. He would just have to be smarter than Tannen—which shouldn't be hard.

"I'll be here at eight," he called back. "I do my killin' after breakfast."

"Marty!" Doc called.

Marty looked over to see the inventor shaking his head. Marty grinned and winked. Didn't Doc remember—by eight o'clock on Monday, they'd be back in 1985!

There was a commotion at the back of the crowd. Marty saw three men pushing their way through—two of them were the deputies who had been guarding the gun table, and the third one also had a badge. Marty had never seen him before—or had he? Holy Cow! This guy had to be Marshal Strickland. He looked exactly like Marty's truant officer, Mr. Strickland, except now he—that is, Strickland's great-grandfather, the marshal—had a handlebar mustache. Whoa. This was heavy.

"What's this about?" the marshal demanded. "You causing trouble here, Tannen?"

"No trouble, Marshal," Tannen replied easily. "Just a little personal matter between me and Eastwood. It don't concern the law."

Strickland shook his head. "Tonight, everything concerns the law. Now break it up. This is a party. Any brawling, it's fifteen days in the county jail."

The crowd started to drift away, and after a bit of tuning up, the band began to play as well.

Strickland glared at both Tannen and Marty—a look that Marty knew all too well—then stalked off toward the festival entrance, his two deputies behind him.

Tannen walked over to Marty.

"Eight o'clock Monday, runt," he demanded as he pointed a finger in Marty's face. "And, if'n you ain't here, I'll hunt you and shoot you down like a duck."

One of the gang members tugged at Tannen's sleeve. "It's 'dog,' Buford. 'Shoot him down like a dog.' "

But Tannen chose to ignore the correction. "Let's go, boys," he said instead, "and let these sissies have their party."

Tannen and his gang turned and swaggered, as a group, toward their horses.

Doc hurried over to Marty's side. "Marty, what are you doing, saying you'll meet Tannen?"

Marty grinned and shrugged. "Hey, Doc, at eight o'clock Monday, we'll be out of here, right?"

But Doc only frowned. "Theoretically, yes," he mused. "But what if the train's late?"

Oh. Marty hadn't thought about that. What with Indian attacks, flash floods, and who knew what else, western trains might not always be exactly on time, would they?

The schoolteacher walked up to him before he could worry anymore.

"Thank you for your gallantry, Clint," Miss Clayton said with a warm smile. "Had you not interceded, Emmett might have been shot."

Well, Marty thought, at least someone was giving him some credit here. Now, if he just wasn't so worried about the train schedule—

"Marty—uh, Clint," Doc barked, breaking the teenager's train of thought. "I'm going to take Clara home. We'll discuss this later."

Doc took Clara's arm and walked away. Maybe, Marty considered, he should get away and think about this, too.

Right now, though, he seemed to be surrounded by some of the locals.

"You sure set him straight, Mr. Eastwood," one of them said jovially.

A second man nodded. "I'm glad somebody's finally got the gumption to stand up to that son of a bitch."

A third fellow pounded him on the back. "You're all right in my book, Mr. Eastwood. I'd like to buy you a drink."

"Uh," Marty replied, a bit overwhelmed, "no thanks—"

That salesman with the loud suit, Elmer Johnson, pushed his way through the crowd and shook Marty's hand. Marty noticed that, in his other hand, Johnson was carrying a gunbelt—and in the belt's holster was the same model pistol Marty had used before.

"Son," Johnson said brightly, "I'd like you to have this brand-new Colt Peacemaker and gunbelt, free of charge." He put the revolver in Marty's right hand, the gunbelt in Marty's left. "I want everybody to know that the gun that killed Buford Tannen was a Colt Peacemaker."

He leaned close to Marty's ear and whispered: " 'Course, you understand that if you lose, I'm takin' it back . . ."

"Uh, thanks," Marty replied, looking down at the gun in his hand. He turned and saw that he was facing Seamus and Maggie McFly.

Great-great-grandfather Seamus shook his head. "You had him, Mr. Eastwood. You could have just walked away, and nobody would have thought the less of you for it. All it would have been was words—hot air from a buffoon." Seamus sighed. "Instead, you let him rile you into playin' his game, his way, by his rules."

But Marty wasn't going to play Tannen's game—but there was no way to tell his great-great-grandfather without explaining all sorts of things that, well, he couldn't explain.

Still, he wanted to reassure the elder McFly. It was the least he could do for family.

"Keep your shirt on, Seamus," Marty answered with a grin. "I know what I'm doing." He shifted his grip on the Colt, ready to twirl it on his finger. Oops. He grabbed the pistol before it fell to the ground. Boy, he had almost forgotten how heavy that sucker was.

It was Maggie's turn to shake her head. She looked at her husband. "He reminds me of poor Martin McFly."

Marty looked up. "Who?"

"My brother, Martin," Seamus answered sadly.

"Wait a minute," Marty interjected. He couldn't believe this. "You have a brother named Martin McFly."

"*Had* a brother," Seamus responded grimly. "Martin used to let men provoke him into fightin', for he was concerned that people would think him a coward if he refused."

Provoked into fighting? Think him a coward? Marty swallowed. Some of this sounded all too familiar.

"That's how he got a Bowie knife shoved

through his belly in a saloon in Virginia City," Seamus continued morosely.

Wow, Marty thought. This was heavier than heavy.

"Never considered the future, poor Martin," Seamus went on balefully, "God rest his soul."

Poor Martin? Marty thought. God rest his soul?

"Sure'n I hope *you're* considerin' the future, Mr. Eastwood," Maggie urged.

"Oh, yeah," Marty answered as honestly as he ever had in all his life. "I think about it all the time."

There were more stars overhead than Doc Brown had ever seen. It was quite remarkable—thousands of points of light, like a field of bright flowers in the sky. Only now did he realize what kind of damage fossil fuels had wrought upon the dull night sky of 1985.

What, however, was even more remarkable was that he now had such a difficult time looking at the stars at all. That was what he and Clara had come out here to do, setting up the now-repaired telescope on its tripod in the back of the buggy. And the stars were quite remarkable. It was only that they paled next to the presence of Clara.

Doc took a deep breath and tried to concentrate on the view through the telescope as Clara continued her explanation.

"And the crater in the middle northwest," she said brightly, "the one that's sort of like a starburst—" Yes. Doc saw it now. "—that's called Copernicus."

She stopped talking, and Doc looked away from the eyepiece. Even in the darkness, he could tell she was blushing.

"Oh, I'm embarrassed," she said with the sweetest smile. "I feel like I'm teaching school."

"No, please," Doc encouraged, "continue the lesson. I've never found lunar geography so fascinating." Or a woman so fascinating, he thought but didn't say aloud. "You're very knowledgeable," he said instead.

Clara tilted her head in that charming way she had, her wonderful smile on her face for good. "When I was eleven years old," she explained, "I had diphtheria and I was quarantined for three months. So my father put this telescope by my bed so that I could see everything out the window. At night I used to stare at the moon. I'd make drawings of it—I even made up my own names for everything. Of course, later I found out all the craters and seas already had names."

What a marvelous story! "And what did you call Copernicus?" Doc asked.

"Little Sunshine," Clara admitted, looking like she might blush all over again.

Doc looked back through the eyepiece of the telescope again. What an appropriate name!

"Yes," he said, "it does look like a little sun."

Clara moved closer to him.

"Emmett," she asked softly as she looked aloft, "do you ever think we'll be able to travel there, the way we travel across the country, on trains?"

Well, this was certainly something he knew about.

"Definitely," he answered quickly, trying to concentrate on the stars, rather than the woman next to him, "although not for another eighty-four years. And not on trains. We'll have space vehicles—capsules, sent aloft with rockets, devices that create giant explosions, explosions so powerful that—"

"—they will break the pull of the earth's gravity," Clara interrupted, "and send the projectile through outer space."

Doc stared at her, dumbfounded. How could she know that sort of thing?

"Emmett," she answered his unspoken question, "I read that book, too. You're quoting Jules Verne: *From the Earth to the Moon*."

Great Scott! Doc couldn't believe it.

"You've read Jules Verne?" he demanded.

"I adore Jules Verne," Clara answered with a little smile.

But this was incredible! What a woman!

"So do I!" Doc agreed, doing his best not to shout. "*Twenty Thousand Leagues Under the Sea*! My absolute favorite! The first time I read that, when I was a little boy, why I wanted to meet Captain Nemo and—"

"Don't tease, Emmett," Clara reprimanded softly as she looked up at him. Somehow, he realized, she had gotten even closer. "You couldn't have read that as a little boy. It was only published about ten years ago!"

"Oh—yes—well." Doc had forgotten exactly where he was. Looking at Clara, he was ready to forget just about anything. "I meant it made me feel like a boy," he explained quickly. But he didn't want to explain anything to anyone. He only wanted to look in Clara's eyes.

"I—I never met a woman who liked—Jules Verne—before," Doc managed somehow.

"I never met a man—like you—before," Clara whispered.

And, without any scientific explanation whatsoever, Emmett Brown moved closer and kissed her full upon the lips.

•Chapter Fourteen•

Sunday, September 6, 1885

Chicken. They were laughing and calling him chicken.

He walked down the dusty street, sarapé over his shoulder, ready for the showdown. Except it wasn't high noon. In fact, he hadn't even had his breakfast.

Still, he had to go through with this. He clamped down on the tiny cigar in the corner of his mouth.

"Aim for the heart, Ramone," he said.

Something was wrong here. These guys were calling Clint Eastwood a chicken!

Somebody clucked.

Marty woke up. All he could see were feathers.

He realized he was staring at the chicken on top of Doc's egg-frying machine, a contraption that managed to break open and fry the egg while making coffee and—there was the ringing now— even setting off an alarm clock.

Marty sat up and turned off the alarm. He was just as glad he was awake. Those western dreams were almost as bad as real life. He rubbed his eyes as he looked around the room.

"Doc?" he called. "Doc?"

There was no answer. Doc wasn't here. Marty wondered if Doc had come home at all last night.

Marty sighed. "I hope you know what you're doing, Doc."

Marty stood up. There in front of him, strapped over a straight-backed chair, were the gun and gunbelt the salesman had given him the night before. Wow, Marty thought. A real Colt Peacemaker—the gun that won the West. He owed it to himself to at least try it on and see how it looked in the light of day.

There was a mirror on the far side of the barn. Once Marty had the gunbelt in place, he sauntered over toward his reflection. The mirror was covered with all sorts of marks and hastily scribbled notes. Doc must be using it for one of his experiments. Still, Marty could see himself well enough between the notations, and—he had to admit—the gunbelt was definitely—heavy.

He drew the gun, then reholstered it. No, it didn't look quite right. He pushed the belt down a little bit on his hips, then stared in the mirror. Yeah. Much better.

"You talkin' to me?" he demanded of his mirror image. "Are you talkin' to me, Tannen?" He glanced to either side before he smirked back in the mirror. "Well, I'm the only one here. You talkin' to me?"

He whipped the gun from its holster.

"Go ahead," he snarled. "Make my day."

It was perfect. Marty had to admit it—not only did he look the part, he was even beginning to feel a little bit like Clint Eastwood.

Still, even his own gun wasn't going to help him if he couldn't get Doc to help them to get back to the future. Where was the inventor, anyway? Maybe, Marty thought, Doc Brown had simply gotten up early and gone out for a morning stroll.

Or, more likely, maybe Doc was getting too involved with the schoolteacher. Marty shook his head. He should be happy that his old friend had found a woman he could really relate to. It was too bad Doc had found her here and now—in 1885, with somebody about to shoot him in the back. He thought again about the words on that tombstone: She had become Doc's "Beloved Clara," even if it meant his death!

Somehow, even with this gun, Marty still felt helpless. Standing around here wasn't going to do him any good, either. Marty decided he would go out and take a look around for Doc.

He walked out of the barn and closed the door behind him. A number of well-dressed townspeople—the men in suits, the women in primly starched dresses—were walking down the main street. Marty realized this was Sunday. Everybody must be going to church.

"Mornin', Mr. Eastwood," one of the local men called as he passed.

Marty waved back at him.

"Top of the mornin' to you, Mr. Eastwood," a second man said as he doffed his hat. "Good luck tomorrow. We'll pray for you."

"Yeah, thanks," Marty replied, managing a smile. Tomorrow. What if he really did have to face Mad Dog Tannen? He knew he could out-think the gunslinger, but could he outdraw him?

Marty smiled and waved as more of the town-folk ambled past. What if—and he had never thought of this before—what if he didn't face the gunslinger? Would Mad Dog Tannen take it out on the townspeople? Marty's hand gripped the handle of the Colt. Carrying a gun brought a real sense of responsibility.

An even more dapper fellow, who was dressed sort of like Abraham Lincoln, in a black suit and stovepipe hat, stopped in front of him.

"Can I interest you in a new suit for tomorrow, Mr. Eastwood?" the newcomer asked in a voice both slow and incredibly deep.

"No, thanks," Marty replied. No need to buy a new suit of clothes when he was leaving town, not to mention the entire era, sometime tomorrow morning. He would face up to Mad Dog Tannen—or run away—in these same old clothes. He wished, though, that the townspeople weren't quite so concerned with his welfare.

But then he saw Doc.

Oh, no. He almost groaned out loud. This was even worse than Marty had imagined.

Great Scott, but life was wonderful!

The sun was so bright, the sky was so blue. His hair was ruffled by a gentle breeze, a warm wind that carried the rhythmic chanting of a thousand insects and the sweet songs of a dozen different species of birds. He didn't think there could be a more perfect day.

And, of course, there was this bunch of flowers in his hand, flowers clasped together by Clara's pin—the one with the large letter *C*. Doc put the bouquet to his nose. He sighed. He didn't think there could be a more perfect bunch of flowers.

"Doc," a young man's voice interrupted, "what are you doing?"

He looked up to see Marty staring at him.

Oh, dear. Doc cleared his throat and stuck the flowers behind his back.

"Huh?" he began, trying to force his brain to consider Marty's question. "Oh, nothing. I was just—out enjoying the morning air." He smiled. "It's lovely here in the morning, don't you think?"

Marty looked up in the sky, but there was a certain air of exasperation in the way he did it, as if he wasn't looking at the beauty so much as, say asking for some heavenly intervention.

"Yeah," the teenager implied impatiently, "real lovely. C'mon, Doc, we gotta get the DeLorean loaded up and ready to roll."

Marty was being a little abrupt. Oh, well, Doc reasoned. He couldn't expect a lad of Marty's tender years to appreciate the depth of Doc's feeling. He turned to follow Marty up the street.

"Doc, look!"

He spun all the way around to see where the teenager was pointing. There, on the far side of the street, was a stonecutter, chiseling away on a brand-new tombstone—a stone with a shape that was very familiar.

The mason had cut two words on the stone: HERE LIES.

Great Scott! That looked very much like the gravestone in the photo—Doc's gravestone!

But perhaps he was jumping to conclusions. This was a very emotional issue, after all. He needed scientific confirmation.

"Marty," he instructed, "let me see that photograph again!"

Marty pulled the photo out of his shirt pocket and handed it to Doc.

Great Scott! The photo had changed!

"My name!" he exclaimed, pointing at the photograph. "It's vanished!"

Marty leaned over to look as Doc once again examined the picture. Yes, the gravestone was the exact same shape as the one across the street, and written on it were HERE LIES and DIED—SEPTEMBER 7, 1885. But now there was a blank space between the two—a space where Doc's name used to be.

"But that's great, Doc!" Marty cheered. "It's gotta be because we're going back to the future tomorrow. It's all being erased!"

No, Doc thought. He wished that were so, but that explanation was too easy.

"Yet only the name is erased," he explained to Marty. "The tombstone itself, and the date, still remain. That doesn't make sense."

But what could this picture be telling him?

"Hmmm," he continued, thinking aloud. "We know that this photograph represents what will happen if the events of today continue to run their course into tomorrow."

"Yeah?" Marty asked. "So?"

So, indeed, Doc agreed. How could he tell Marty, gently, what he had just realized?

The teenager jumped as Mr. Phipps stuck a tape measure next to his leg.

"Excuse me, Mr. Eastwood," Phipps said, doffing his stovepipe hat. "Just want to take your measurements."

"Hey!" Marty objected. "I told you I don't want a new suit!"

New suit? Oh, dear, Doc thought. Didn't Marty know who this fellow was?

"Oh," Mr. Phipps, the local undertaker, answered with his all-too-pleasant smile. "This isn't for a suit. This is for your coffin."

Marty turned rather pale.

"My—coffin?" he asked, his voice cracking with surprise.

The undertaker nodded smartly as he stretched his measuring tape across Marty's shoulders. "Odds are running two to one against you," he added jovially. He pulled a pencil and notebook from the inner pocket of his black frock coat and rapidly jotted down a list of numbers. "Might as well be prepared."

Phipps replaced the notebook and pencil within his coat, doffed his hat again, then hurried down the street, whistling cheerfully.

Doc Brown bit his lower lip. He supposed that Phipps had, in his rather direct way, made it easier for Doc to break the news.

Doc pointed back at the snapshot, then looked straight at Marty. "So it may not be *my* name that's supposed to end up on this tombstone. It may be yours."

Marty glanced down at the picture. He looked even paler than before.

"Great Scott!" he whispered.

•Chapter
Fifteen•

Doc Brown had never seen his teenage friend so shaken before. But he also noticed something else, something very disturbing, that he hadn't seen in his previously lovestruck moment.

"Marty," Doc demanded, pointing at the belt hanging from the teenager's jeans, "why are you wearing that gun? You're not considering going up against Tannen tomorrow?"

Marty glanced a little guiltily down at the weapon at his side. When his gaze met Doc's again, he shrugged and tried to smile.

"Hey, Doc," he explained, "tomorrow I'm going back to the future, with you." He patted the gun handle self-consciously. "But if Tannen comes looking for trouble, I'm gonna be ready." He stood up straight, squaring his shoulders, ready for an imaginary gunfight. "You heard what he called me last night."

Oh, yes, Doc Brown remembered now. Marty did always react badly to being called chicken or yellow or scaredy cat or any of those things. It was the one failing of a very bright lad. Doc was certainly glad he was older and more experienced. It wouldn't do to have two of them with such failings—especially in a crisis. But how could he get Marty to see the error of his ways?

"Marty," he replied sternly, "you can't lose all sense of judgment just because someone calls you a name. That's exactly what causes you to get into that accident in the future that—"

"What?" Marty interrupted. "What about my future?"

Oh, dear. Doc Brown realized, a bit too late, that he shouldn't have mentioned that incident in 1985, when Marty's new Four-by-Four got into an accident—Well, would get into an accident, really—with that Rolls Royce. It was all the result of a stupid drag race, down near Hilldale. The teenager had gotten pretty banged up, and then the owner of the Rolls had sued—the whole thing hadn't been very pretty, and it had broken not only Marty's hand, but his spirit, too. The teenager had gotten so depressed—would get so depressed, Doc reminded himself—that he had even given up playing the guitar.

And now Doc had blabbed Marty's future right to Marty. Maybe, Doc considered, Emmett L. Brown did have a fault or two.

The teenager watched him intently, expecting an answer.

"I can't tell you," Doc admitted. "It might make things worse." Like creating another paradox, Doc thought. And that was one thing they didn't need—things were confusing enough already.

"Worse?" Marty yelled. "Wait a minute, Doc, what's wrong with my future?"

But Doc had said too much already.

"Marty, we all have to make decisions that affect the course of our lives." Doc nodded sadly to himself. "You've gotta do what you've gotta do."

He reached in his pocket to curl his fingers around the flowers. Clara. What was he going to do with Clara?

After a moment, he added: "And I've gotta do what I've gotta do."

Marty and Doc had finally agreed to go through with the plan. So why did Marty feel like something was going to go wrong?

They had waited until nightfall. Then they had loaded up the DeLorean onto Doc's oversized wagon, hitched up the team, and driven out of town. Doc had modified the DeLorean slightly the day before, replacing its rubber tires with metal wheels properly gauged to run on the train tracks. Once they had driven the wagon out to the rail spur that led to the ravine, they pushed the DeLorean off the wagon and onto a special set of tracks Doc had devised to guide the car over the tailgate and onto the actual train line.

Everything was going exactly according to plan. So why was Marty so nervous? Maybe it had something to do with the way Doc was acting. The inventor kept talking to himself. Sometimes, he would look quickly at Marty, then just as rapidly glance away. And every once in a while, his old friend seemed to forget completely what he was doing, and just sit and stare into space until Marty reminded him what they were working on.

And, then again, there was that business about the future—Marty's future—that Doc had started to talk about before he clammed up. What could be so terrible that Doc would act like that? Not that, Marty reminded himself again, Doc was acting normal anyway. The inventor was probably worrying about those time paradoxes, where the past couldn't happen because somebody wasn't in the right place at the right time. Marty gave up. He couldn't do anything about it now, anyway. Before he could worry about the future, Marty had to get out of the past.

Besides that, Doc was looking at him again. This time, for a change, the inventor didn't look away, although—from the grim look on Doc's face—Marty half wished he would.

"Marty, I've made a decision," Doc said rapidly. "I'm not going with you tomorrow. I'm staying here."

Marty shook his head. This didn't make any sense at all. "What are you talkin' about, Doc?"

"There's no point denying it," the inventor added firmly. "I'm in love with Clara. You were right about this man-woman thing. I can't explain it, but I just know that"—Doc took a deep breath—"she's the one." He pounded his fist on the edge of the wagon. "She even likes Jules Verne, Marty! She has all of his books!"

Oh, no. Marty was afraid something like this was going to happen. There had to be some way he could still talk Doc out of it!

"But, Doc, we don't belong here, neither one of us. It still could be *you* that gets killed tomorrow." He pulled out the photo again and waved it under Doc's nose. "What if this *is* your future?"

But the inventor was adamant. "Marty, the future isn't written. It can be changed. You know that. Anyone can make their future whatever they want it to be."

He pushed the photograph, and Marty's hand, away. "I can't let this one little photograph determine my entire destiny. I have to live my life according to what I believe is right"—he put his right hand upon his chest—"in my heart."

Yep. Doc had really gone loopy—completely off the deep end. But didn't he remember the reason Marty was here in the first place—to rescue him from Mad Dog Tannen and all?

"Hey, Doc," Marty spoke again, choosing his words carefully. "I'm all for—true love and everything, and I like Clara, too. Really, you and her, you're—kinda cute together. And, if this were 1985, I'd say go for it."

He sighed. He couldn't put it any better than this. "But it's 1885, Doc." He pointed at the inventor. "*You're* the Doc. So tell me. What's the right thing to do"—he pointed to Doc's forehead—"up here?"

Doc blinked, then sighed, then nodded—he knew Marty was right. He reached past the teenager to pull the release lever on the side of the wagon. The DeLorean ran down the temporary rails onto the train track.

"I'll be back in an hour or two, Marty," Doc said sadly. "I've at least got to tell her good-bye."

Marty shook his head. The inventor wasn't thinking straight. "Doc, you can't. What are you gonna say? 'I've gotta go back to the future?' If you tell her the truth, she'll think you're lying. And if you lie to her, well—" Marty sighed again. "There's just no way you can make her understand this thing."

But Doc was being as stubborn as ever. "She'll understand, Marty," he insisted. "I know she will."

"No, she won't, Doc," Marty replied softly. "Hell, I'm in it with you and I barely understand it myself." It was an impossible situation. What could they do? Marty certainly never would have left Jennifer behind.

Maybe, Marty realized, Doc needed to do the same kind of thing.

"Look, Doc," Marty suggested, "maybe, well— I don't know if it's a violation of all that space-time stuff, but maybe we could take Clara with us?"

"To the future?" Doc asked, quite startled by the idea.

Marty nodded.

Doc frowned and shook his head. "As you re-minded me, Marty, I'm a scientist, so I must be scientific about this. I cautioned you about disrupting the continuum for your own personal benefit. Therefore, I must do no less." He took a deep, but ragged, breath. "We shall proceed as planned. And as soon as we return to 1985"—he walked over to the DeLorean and rested his hand upon the car's sleek, black finish—"we'll destroy this infernal machine. Traveling through time has become much too painful."

Marty nodded again. Everything that had happened since he'd gotten into the DeLorean had been one long, never-ending mess. This, at least, was one thing both he and Doc could agree on.

Great Scott!

He had to do it. No matter what rational explanations Marty gave him, there were simply times a man had to listen to his own heart.

Once the DeLorean was set up on the train tracks, and in its proper place for the following morning, he and Marty had finished setting up camp, and, after a campfire meal of beans and beef jerky—which, quite frankly, was still not quite sitting right in Doc's stomach—they had unrolled their bedrolls in preparation for sleep. Marty had drifted right off. With the amount of work they had done, Doc should have fallen into an exhausted sleep as well—but he couldn't. His eyes wouldn't stay closed. His mind kept returning to Clara. He had to see her one more time.

He had to say good-bye.

He stood up at last, careful not to disturb Marty, and crept to where his horse was tied at the edge of camp.

Doc saw the light burning in Clara's window as he rode up. He dismounted, and as he tied Archimedes to the old oak tree in the schoolteacher's front yard, he realized he could see Clara as well. She was sitting there in the rocking chair, reading by lamplight. She had let her hair down, and it hung to her shoulders, hiding her delicate features in shadow. Doc could even see the title of the book: Jules Verne's *Twenty Thousand Leagues Under the Sea*—the book Doc had said was his favorite.

She looked so beautiful at that moment, caught in quiet contemplation. Doc wished again there was some way he could stay, some way they could spend the rest of their lives together. But it still seemed quite impossible.

He had to finish this. He quickly climbed onto the porch and rapped on the front door.

Clara turned and glanced out the window. She smiled when she saw Doc. Doc felt an ache deep inside his chest when he saw that smile for what he knew would be the last time. Clara put down her book and jumped from her chair to answer the door.

Doc swallowed as the front door opened.

"Why, Emmett," Clara began sweetly—and hers was the sweetest voice Doc had ever heard. "This is a most unexpected pleasure. Won't you come in?"

Oh, dear. Now that he was here, Doc could feel his resolve weaken. If he walked into the schoolteacher's house tonight, he didn't think he would ever leave again.

"N-no," he stammered, "I'd better not—I—"

Clara's smile transformed into a look of deepest concern. "What's wrong?"

Doc couldn't hold it back any longer. It was better to come out with it and get this whole thing over with. Somehow, though, it almost sounded as if somebody else were talking when he said the words: "I've come to say good-bye."

"Good-bye?" Clara smiled uncertainly. "Where are you going?"

Doc took a deep breath. He had to finish this now, or he would never again find the strength to end it.

"I'm going away, and"—how could he say it?—"well, I'm afraid I'll never see you again."

Clara took a step back, her hand at her throat. "Emmett!"

Oh, he couldn't stand to see the love of his life hurt like this. But what could he say or do to make it any better?

"Clara," he said evenly, "I want you to know that I care about you deeply. But I've realized that I don't belong here and I have to go back where I came from."

Clara took the hand away from her throat. "And where might that be?" she asked cautiously.

Doc sighed. Marty was right. It had come down to this.

"I can't tell you," he replied.

Clara nodded and took a step forward, as if she had made a decision. "Then, wherever you're going, take me with you."

Doc bit his lip. Marty had been more than right. This was just too painful.

"I can't, Clara. I wish it didn't have to be this way, but just believe me when I tell you that I'll never forget you and that—I love you."

But Clara couldn't leave it at that. "And, Emmett, I love you," she said firmly. "But I don't understand what you're trying to say."

Doc spread his hands, his fingers curling as if they might find an answer out in the night air.

"Clara," he said, softly and hopelessly, "I don't think there's any way you *can* understand it."

The schoolteacher stepped even closer, so that she was looking right at him, only a foot away.

"Please, Emmett," she insisted. "I have to know. If you sincerely do love me, tell me the truth."

Well, Doc thought, if that's what she wanted, how could he deny her? How, indeed, could he deny her anything?

"All right then," he replied evenly. "I'm from—the future. I came here in a time machine that I invented, and tomorrow, I have to go back to the year 1985."

He stopped, waiting for her disbelieving reply.

But she nodded instead.

"Yes, Emmett, I do understand."

She did? She could actually accept that he came from the future, and that he had to go back? Then

Marty had been wrong! Doc should have known that an exceptional woman like Clara, with all those fine qualities, couldn't possibly—

"I understand that," Clara continued rapidly, "because you know I'm partial to the writings of Jules Verne, that you concocted those mendacities in the expectation that you could take advantage of me one last time."

And with that, she slapped him, hard across the face.

Doc blinked, stunned by the force of the blow.

"Oh," Clara went on, the anger rising in her voice, "I've heard some whoppers in my day, but the fact that you would expect me to entertain a notion like that is so degrading and insulting—"

She stopped for a second to take a quick breath before she launched into Doc again. "All you had to say was 'I don't love you and I don't want to see you anymore.' That at least would have been respectful."

She stepped back, slamming the door in Doc's face.

"But that's not the truth!" Doc called to the wooden barrier. But there was no response, except, perhaps, for a soft sobbing sound from inside the schoolteacher's house.

Doc turned and staggered back to his horse.

What else was there to live for?

"What'll it be, Emmett?" the bartender called cheerfully. "The usual?"

How could the barkeep be so cheerful? It was

amazing, in a way, that other people could smile when Doc Emmett L. Brown's world had ended.

"No, Chester," Doc replied. He had made his decision before he had even stepped into the Palace Saloon. "I need something a lot stronger tonight."

The bartender nodded. "Sasparilla?" he suggested.

Doc shook his head. He had made it to the bar. It was time to drink his troubles away.

"Whiskey," he demanded.

The bartender's smile disappeared. "Whiskey? Emmett, no, you can't. Remember what happened to you on the Fourth of July—"

But Doc wouldn't be talked out of it. He had thought about this over and over again as he had ridden Archimedes back into town: If he couldn't mend his broken heart, he would try to wash it away.

"Whiskey, Chester," he repeated solemnly.

The bartender whistled softly. "I hope you know what you're doing, Emmett." He reached behind the bar for the whiskey bottle.

A fellow in a checkered suit and derby hat—undoubtedly one of those salesmen that were always passing through town—shook his head where he stood farther down the bar.

"It's a woman, right?" he called to Doc.

Chester poured him a shot. Doc nodded his head.

"I knew it," the salesman said to a fellow next to him dressed in pretty much the same style as the man who was speaking. "I've seen that look on a man's face a thousand times, all over the country." He looked back at Doc. "All I can tell you, friend, is that you'll get over her."

Get over her? What could this fellow in the checkered suit really know about true love? Doc stared down at the shot glass filled with whiskey.

"Nope," he replied. "Clara was one in a million. One in a billion. One in a googol-plex." A sigh escaped from somewhere deep inside. "The woman of my dreams, and I've lost her for all time." Doc put his fingers around the shot glass.

The first fellow in plaid moved down the bar toward Doc. "I can assure you, sir," he said, his voice somehow both jovial and full of concern, "that there *are* other women. If peddlin' barbwire all across this land has taught me one thing for certain, it's that you never know what the future might bring."

"The future?" He let go of the glass. He could fill these fellows in on a thing or two. "Oh, I can tell you about the future—"

He would forget about Clara one way or another. Doc started to talk.

Marty opened his eyes. The sky above was clear and blue. It looked like it was going to be a beautiful morning. He sat up and stretched.

"Man, I slept like a rock," he called out. "What time is it, Doc?"

There was no answer.

"Doc?"

Marty looked around. Doc was nowhere to be

seen. And what was worse, Doc's bedroll didn't even look like it had been slept in.

Marty stood up. There was no sign of Doc anywhere. And one of the horses was gone.

"No," Marty said aloud, "not again!" What had Doc gone off and done this time? He had a sudden, terrible thought. What if Doc had already gone and gotten shot?

Marty pulled the photograph out of his pocket. No, the picture was the same, or at least it hadn't changed any more. HERE LIES and the date of death were still there, with no name in between. So Doc was still all right, at least for the moment. But for how long? And what if Mad Dog Tannen ran into the inventor before Marty could find him?

Marty decided he'd better get into town to look for his friend. If he didn't find him soon, Doc might not have much of a future at all.

Doc didn't know how long he'd been talking. He didn't even know, really, why he was talking in the first place. At least, if he talked, he didn't have to think about how he had lost Clara and ruined his life. Yes, that was it exactly—more talking, less thinking.

He looked back and forth at the crowd that had gathered at either end of the bar. "We don't need horses," he informed them all, "because we have motorized carriages called automobiles."

He looked down at his whiskey glass. He still hadn't gotten around to taking a drink. That was a problem with all this talking—it was difficult to simultaneously pontificate and drink yourself into oblivion. Well, Doc would change all that. He would take his first drink right now.

But Jeb, one of the old-time locals, scratched at his drooping black mustache as he asked a question. "Well, if everybody's got all these automo-what's its, don't anybody walk or run anymore?"

"Of course we run," Doc answered, deciding he could leave the whiskey for another second. "But for recreation. For fun."

"Run for fun?" Jeb asked incredulously. "Now, where's the fun in that? What's wrong, don't they have women anymore?"

Doc sighed. Maybe this was just too difficult to explain. Maybe he should take that drink after all.

"Or gambling?" Jeb added.

Doc put down the glass.

"We have gambling. But it's all in a town called Las Vegas."

"Haw!" laughed Zeke, another of the old-timers. "I been to Las Vegas." He scratched at his snow-white beard. "Ain't nothin' there but desert. No water, not even a saloon."

"Next thing you're gonna tell us," interrupted a third fellow named Levi as he pushed up his derby hat, "is ain't nobody got guns no more neither."

Doc nodded knowingly. "Oh, we still have guns."

"Thank God there's *some*thing civilized about the place!" Jeb exclaimed.

Doc looked back down at his whiskey.

"You know," the bartender remarked to one of the salesmen, "I ain't heard anybody spin a yarn this wild since that Missouri feller come through here a few years back, what was his name? Twain? Or was it—Clemens?"

Zeke leaned over the bar. "How many has he had?" he asked the bartender.

"None," the barkeep replied with a shake of his head. "That's his first one, and he still ain't touched it yet."

Doc looked down at his glass. Yep, he thought. It was just about time to take a drink.

Meanwhile, at a campsite just beyond the outskirts of town, Buford Tannen kicked his sleeping sidekicks awake.

"Let's go," Tannen demanded, pausing a moment to spit. "I got me a runt to kill."

One of his men sat up, rubbed his eyes, and lit a cigar.

"It's still early, boss," he mentioned. "What's your hurry?"

Buford grinned as he patted his revolver.

"I'm hungry," he drawled.

Even though they were barely awake, all three men knew enough to laugh.

•Chapter Sixteen•

Marty jumped off his horse and ran into the blacksmith shop.

"Doc?" he called. "Yo, Doc!"

No one answered back. The barn was empty. Doc had sent the remaining horses to graze in a local farmer's field, just in case he and Marty really didn't come back. The place was totally silent, the blacksmith's fire out, the tools neatly placed back on their hooks and shelves. The place didn't looked lived-in anymore, and it certainly didn't look like Doc had been back through here.

But where could he be? Marty had already stopped at the schoolteacher's home on the edge of town, but there had been nobody there. Where could he look next? Or had Mad Dog Tannen already gotten to Doc, somewhere outside of town?

Marty walked out of the barn and saw what

looked like Doc's horse, tied up in front of the Palace Saloon. Marty trotted quickly down the street. Yep, that was Archimedes all right; Marty would recognize those brown and white markings anywhere. But what would Doc be doing in a saloon?

He could hear voices inside as he ran toward the Palace's swinging doors. And one of the voices was Doc's!

Marty walked into the saloon and saw his friend surrounded by a couple dozen locals, all paying total attention to whatever the inventor was talking about.

"Doc!" Marty called. "What are you doing?"

Doc looked sadly at his teenage friend. "I've lost her, Marty. Lost her for all time."

Oh, no. It was Clara again. Marty sighed. They didn't have time for Clara anymore.

"C'mon, Doc," he insisted. "You've gotta come back with me!"

"Where?" Doc asked miserably.

Did Marty dare remind Doc in front of all these people? He had to—there was no time for anything else!

"Back to the future," Marty said.

"All right," Doc said, resigned to his fate. "Might as well. There's nothing left for me here." He nodded to the old-timers at the bar. "Gentlemen, excuse me, but my friend and I have to catch a train."

The old-timers nearest to Doc all raised their glasses in a salute.

"Here's to you, blacksmith!" the fellow with the derby called.

"And to the future!" added the fellow with the mustache.

"Amen!" the guy with the snow-white beard concluded.

The three drank.

"Amen," Doc replied as he lifted up his shot glass and drank as well.

"Emmett, no!" the bartender called as Doc drank, but the whiskey was already gone, swallowed in a single gulp.

Doc smiled and put down his glass. He took a step toward Marty. Somehow, his foot never quite hit the floor.

Instead, Doc fell flat on his face.

Marty ran to his side. "Doc, Doc, wake up!"

Marty knelt down and shook the shoulders of his friend. Doc Brown grunted, then made another noise that might have been snoring.

Marty looked up and saw a clock behind the bar. The clock read 7:45. It was almost eight o'clock!

"How much has he had?" Marty asked the bartender.

"Just that one," the bartender replied with a shake of his head. "The man just can't hold his liquor."

Marty stood up. "Coffee!" he ordered. "Black!"

He looked out the window. The street beyond was empty. There was no sign yet of Mad Dog Tannen and his mob. But Marty had a perfect view of the new clock-tower clock, still on its wagon.

7:45, the clock said.

Don't remind me, Marty thought.

They were running out of time.

Clara had had enough.

She had come west to start a new life. She wanted to see new things, meet new people, and forget some of those unfortunate events that had happened to her back east. What a fool she had been. It was absurd, really, to think that people would be any different out here; to think that Emmett would be any different from all those other men she had met over the years. It was so absurd that she could almost laugh. Except, if she let any of her emotions out, she would probably start to cry.

She hefted her suitcase up onto the train platform and walked quickly to the ticket window. The train agent looked up and nodded pleasantly.

"I'd like to buy a ticket on the next train, please," Clara said quickly.

"To where, ma'am?" the ticket agent asked.

"Anywhere," she replied. "As long as it's far away from here."

The agent arched an eyebrow and looked down at his schedule. "Well, the Number Nineteen to Sacramento should be arriving in about ten minutes. It leaves at eight."

Clara looked at the clock on the wall behind the ticket agent. It read 7:45. Fifteen minutes, then, and she could leave Hill Valley and Emmett L.

Brown and Jules Verne and square dancing and all the stars in the nighttime sky—she could leave everything behind.

"That'll be just fine," she answered in an even voice. Fifteen minutes, and Hill Valley would be nothing but memories.

And maybe, someday, she could forget those as well.

Marty rolled Doc onto his back, then managed to prop him up to a sitting position as the bartender fetched the coffee. The barkeep walked around the end of the bar and handed Marty a steaming mug.

Marty put the coffee cup to Doc's lips. Marty tilted the cup slightly. Doc took a sip and made a face as more of the coffee sloshed down his chin. He started to snore all over again.

"Son," the bartender said over Marty's shoulder, "if you want him to sober up fast, you're gonna need something a little stronger than coffee."

Marty looked up at the barkeep. In matters like this, he supposed, he should consult the expert.

"What do you suggest?" he asked.

The bartender grinned and waved a young man over to the bar.

"Joey," he instructed, "get me some tabasco sauce, cayenne pepper, onion, chili peppers, and mustard seed."

The young fellow nodded and ran into the back room as the bartender reached beneath the polished wooden shelf and pulled out a bottle of vinegar and part of an onion. His helper rushed back with an armful of jars and bottles and dumped them on the bar. The bartender whistled tunelessly as he mixed all of it in a beer glass, then glanced up at Marty.

"In a few minutes," the barkeep remarked cheerfully, "he'll be as sober as a priest on Sunday."

Marty glanced at the clock by the bartender's shoulder. It read 7:47.

"Ten minutes!" Marty muttered. "Why do we have to cut these things so damned close?"

The bartender leaned over the bar, handing Marty both the glass, which was now filled with a uniform vile brown liquid, and a clothespin.

"Put the clothespin over his nose," the bartender instructed. "When he opens his mouth, pour it down his gullet. Then stand back."

Marty did as he was told, placing the clothespin over the bridge of Doc's nose, effectively closing off his nasal passages. The sleeping Doc opened his mouth to gulp in air. In a single, fluid motion, Marty poured the contents of the glass into Doc's gullet.

What happened next was quite amazing. In fact, Marty couldn't figure out what was more incredible—the strength of Doc's bloodcurdling scream, the amazingly bloodred color of his face, or the speed with which he ran from the bar to dunk his head in the horse trough.

Well, no matter which was more surprising, the final effect was quite dramatic. Marty and the barkeep both ran out of the bar to find Doc's head totally submerged in water!

Marty heard a gulping sound from the trough, and realized that Doc must be drinking water. He hoped, when this was all over, that his friend would forgive him for this dramatic cure.

Doc stood, took a deep breath, and fell on his face!

"That was just the reflex action," the bartender explained. "It'll take a few more minutes for the stuff to clear up his head."

The bartender grabbed Doc's arms while Marty took his legs. Together, they started to drag him back indoors.

Marty glanced over at the courthouse clock. It was 7:49. Marty realized that if they didn't get going soon, there wouldn't be time for anybody to forgive anything.

But there were others out this morning who didn't want to forgive anything, ever.

Marshal Strickland urged his horse forward, and his son followed his lead. There were Mad Dog and his boys, just like Strickland had expected, riding in toward Hill Valley. The marshal's horse walked out from behind the cover of the pine trees. His son's mount came out next. Strickland made sure that Buford and his boys could see the shotgun on the marshal's lap.

"That's far enough, Tannen," he called out. "I don't want any trouble."

But Tannen only grinned.

"Stay out of my way," he drawled, "and there won't be none."

Strickland reached down for his shotgun. "I'm warnin' you—"

Tannen whipped out his pistol and shot the gun out of Strickland's hands. The shotgun flew into the bushes, half a dozen feet away. Strickland stared at Tannen. He had never seen anybody that fast on the draw!

Buford had turned his pistol on the boy. "Drop it, sonny," he ordered.

But Strickland's son still clutched his own shotgun. He looked over to his father, a silent question in his eyes.

What could Strickland do? Tannen had the drop on them. He didn't want to see his boy killed.

"Do it, son," Strickland said.

"Yes, Pa." His boy tossed his shotgun onto the ground.

"Now, I'm warnin' *you*, Marshal," Tannen continued in that same low-key voice. "I'm here on a personal matter. And if you want to live to see your boy grow up, you just ride outta here for a few hours and leave me be!"

The rest of Tannen's gang had drawn their guns now, too. Marshal Strickland saw four pistols, all aimed at his chest.

He had no choice. He had to leave. He sighed and turned his horse around to leave.

Tannen watched the horse walk away for a moment, then raised his gun and shot the marshal in the back.

Strickland fell from his horse.

"I lied, Marshal," Tannen remarked amiably. He waved for his boys to follow him into town. They all knew they had some important killing to do.

The boy jumped from his horse and ran to his fallen father.

"Pa!" he called. "Pa!"

But Marshal Strickland could barely hear him. He turned to his son and, with his last breath, whispered: "Remember that word, son: Discipline!"

"I will, Pa," the boy promised. If he had his way, it would be a word that every Strickland would live by, for generations!

•Chapter
Seventeen•

Between Marty and the bartender, they managed to get Doc back indoors and propped up in a chair. Doc seemed to be more or less awake, but had once again lost control of all his muscles. Marty looked at the clock over the bar. It ticked from 7:49 to 7:50.

It was time to get serious. Marty slapped his friend across the face.

"C'mon, Doc. Get sober!"

Doc's head lolled to the other side.

Marty looked up as he heard the hinge creak on the swinging doors.

"Hello, Seamus," the bartender called. "Didn't expect to see you here this morning."

Marty realized he had been holding his breath. He half expected the next person through that door to be Mad Dog Tannen with his pistol drawn. Instead, it was his great-great-grandfather. Marty grinned at Seamus, and his ancestor smiled back.

"Well," Seamus said uncertainly, "something inside me told me I should be here. As if my future had something to do with it—"

But Marty's future was already being planned, outside the Palace Saloon.

Buford Tannen and his three men pulled up to the hitching post in front of the saloon. They dismounted and tied up their horses. The streets were deserted. Everyone knew what was due to happen this morning.

Tannen walked down the dusty street until he was opposite the swinging doors of the Palace.

"All right, runt!" he yelled. "It's eight o'clock, and I'm calling you out!"

Marty looked up. The saloon was as still as death. The clock read 7:51.

"Just my luck!" Marty whispered. "He's early!"

What could he do? One thing for sure, he wasn't going to go out until it was time.

"It's not eight o'clock yet!" he yelled toward the door.

"It is by my watch!" Tannen yelled back. "Now, let's settle this thing once and for all, Eastwood—or ain't you got the gumption?"

Marty took a breath. Now that the time had come for the showdown, Marty realized he didn't want to shoot anyone—even Buford "Mad Dog"

Tannen. But how did he get out of this? And what happened if he couldn't?

Marty reached in his pocket. He had to sneak a peak at the photograph.

The photo had changed again. HERE LIES was still there, along with the date of death—today's date. But there was a name now between the two, the letters faint, as if washed away by the rain and winds of time. Marty started to squint, but the letters seemed to grow clearer with every passing second, until he could read them easily: CLINT EASTWOOD.

Oh, no! Marty stuffed the photo back in his pocket and looked up to see Seamus McFly staring at him. Seamus, the same man who had told Marty he could have walked away from this fight, had come back here again. Seamus had said something about feeling like he had to be here, like the future depended on it. Could he be here to keep Marty from fighting again?

Marty decided it was worth a try. "Hey, listen!" he called out the door. "The truth is, I—uh—I don't really feel up to this, so I forfeit."

"Forfeit?" Tannen blurted to his men outside. "What's that mean?"

"Means you win without a fight," one of his men answered him.

"Without shootin'?" Buford screamed. "He can't do that!

"You know what I think?" Tannen called in to Marty. "I think you ain't nothin' but a gutless, yellow turd." Buford's boys laughed at that one.

"And I'm givin' you to the count of ten to come out here and prove I'm wrong!

"One!" Tannen began.

Somehow, Marty and Doc had to get out of here. But Doc was still in his stupor. Marty slapped him again.

"C'mon, Doc!" he pleaded. "Sober up! Please!"

"Two!" came the voice from outside.

Marty felt a hand on his shoulder. He looked up to see one of the old-timers.

"Get out there, son," the old fellow with the derby advised. "I got twenty dollars' gold bet on you, so don't let me down."

"Three!" Tannen yelled.

The old-timer with the white beard shuffled over to stand next to the first. "I got me thirty dollars' gold bet agin' you, so don't let me down, neither."

Thirty dollars? Marty blinked. Some of the townspeople were betting *against* him?

"Four!"

The third old-timer, the one with the black mustache, joined the first two. "You might as well face it, son," he said sagely. " 'Cause if you don't go out there—"

"Five!" Tannen's voice interrupted.

Marty had had just about enough of this.

"What?" he called up to the old-timers. "What happens if I don't go out there?"

By now, the rest of the crowd had moved forward to gather behind the old cowboys. They were the ones that answered Marty.

"You're a coward," a fellow with an eyepatch said.

"Six!" Mad Dog interjected.

"And you'll be branded a coward," a fellow who didn't seem to have any teeth whistled, "for the rest of your days!"

"Everyone everywhere'll say that Clint Eastwood is the biggest yellow belly in the West!" the oldster with the derby concluded.

"So, here—" The guy with an eyepatch pulled out his pistol and put it on the table in front of Marty.

"Seven!"

Marty looked down at the gun, then up at the faces of all the men watching him. The way they were staring, it was apparent they didn't like cowards.

"I've already got a gun," Marty explained.

"Then let's see you use it!" somebody else yelled.

"Eight!"

Marty looked down at the Colt strapped to his belt. He thought of the photo of the tombstone. They all wanted him to go out there and die like a man.

"Nine!"

Marty's gaze wandered to the edge of the group and saw Seamus McFly. No, everyone didn't want him to go out there. Seamus wanted Marty to make his own decision. And Seamus had told him that a real man didn't always go out and blindly fight. A real man was somebody who could make real decisions about what was best for him.

"Ten!" Tannen yelled.

Marty had made up his mind. He stood and looked at the other men in the saloon.

"Hey," he said forcefully, "this is ridiculous! I don't care what Tannen says! He's an idiot! And I don't care what anybody else says either!"

He looked over to Seamus. His great-great-grandfather smiled, nodding his approval.

Doc sat up, blinking rapidly.

Marty turned back to his friend. "Doc! Are you all right!"

The inventor looked around, trying to get his bearings.

"I think so," he said after a moment's pause. "Whew!" He rubbed his head. "What a headache! I confess, the one thing I really miss here is Tylenol."

Marty let out a long breath. Now that Doc was all right, they could get away from this place and back to the DeLorean.

"Bartender," he asked, "is there another way out of here?"

The barkeep pointed to a door at the far end of the bar. "Through the back."

Marty leaned over and helped Doc to his feet.

"Do you hear me?" Buford Tannen screamed outside. "I said that's *ten*, you gutless yellow turd!"

The others in the saloon shook their heads and started to talk among themselves.

"Tannen's right," the old fellow with the derby muttered. "The runt's yellow."

"He's got about as much guts as a snake has hips," the white-bearded oldster added.

"The most sickening display of cowardice I have ever seen," the senior with the mustache agreed.

Seamus stepped forward. "Is that so? Well, I say there's a difference between being a coward and being a fool. No, sir, I'd say that young fella's got a noggin full of horse sense, he does."

He grinned at Marty again. "Good luck to ye, Mr. Eastwood."

Marty waved back as he helped Doc through the door.

"Good luck to you, too!"

Doc shook off Marty's helping hand as they walked down the short back hall toward a second door. Marty opened the door and saw they were in an alleyway on the side of the saloon. Well, if they could move fast enough and grab their horses, maybe the element of surprise would give them a chance to get away.

Marty started running. So did Doc, but the inventor wasn't quite as sure on his feet as he had thought. He stumbled, falling with a crash into a pile of cans and wooden boxes.

One of Tannen's men ran around the corner and saw both Doc and Marty.

"Hey!" the gunman yelled.

A bullet whistled past Marty's ear.

Marty realized it wasn't over yet.

•Chapter Eighteen•

Marty ran across the street, diving into the open door of a cabinet shop and right into a cast-iron, potbellied stove. His left shoulder rammed the door, knocking it from its hinges. It clanged as it hit the floor.

Ow. You had to be careful when you got involved in this western action stuff. Marty massaged his shoulder. There would be a real bruise there, but nothing was broken. He was lucky he didn't hit the stove with his head. He would have passed out and had another one of those Clint Eastwood dreams.

Dreams? Marty looked down at the solid iron stove door. He smiled just like Clint Eastwood.

He took a deep breath and realized he was in here by himself. What had happened to Doc?

"Listen up, Eastwood!" Tannen yelled from

somewhere outside. "I aim to shoot somebody today. I'd prefer it be you. But if you're just too damn yellow, then it'll have to be your blacksmith friend."

Oh, no! Marty crept over to the window and cautiously peeked above the sill. There, in the middle of the street, were two of Tannen's gunmen, holding on to Doc, and Mad Dog Tannen, pointing a pistol straight at Doc's ear.

"Marty!" Doc yelled when he saw his friend. "Forget about me and save yourself!"

That was one thing Marty knew he could never do. Tannen had finally accomplished what he had wanted all along. Marty was going to have to face him.

Marty pulled the snapshot from his pocket one more time. There were two names there now— CLINT EASTWOOD and EMMETT L. BROWN—both on the tombstone, one over the other, as if the picture had been taken twice. It looked like somebody was going to die, but who? Was this his future, or Doc's?

"You got one minute to decide!" Tannen yelled outside.

Marty could hear the train whistle in the distance—the train that would have taken Doc and Marty to the future—and now a train that one or maybe both of them would never see.

The train arrived right on schedule—and not a moment too soon for Clara. As soon as a pair of passengers had disembarked, she climbed aboard and walked down the car until she found a seat.

A pair of men in loud, checked suits sat across from her—some of those salesmen that were always passing through Hill Valley. One of them was telling a long-winded story about some fellow he'd had some drinks with—apparently all night long. Clara turned away from them and looked out the window, hoping that would be enough to discourage either of the gentlemen from including her in the conversation. The way she felt right now, she didn't want to talk to anyone.

"All aboaarrrrdddddd!" the conductor yelled at the end of the car. The train lurched forward, then slowly picked up speed as it pulled away from the Hill Valley station.

The fellow across from her was talking very loudly, as if everything he said was part of his salesman's spiel.

"Yessir, that poor feller last night had the worst case of broken heart I have ever seen," he chattered on. "And when he said he didn't know how he'd get through the rest of his life, knowing how much he'd hurt his poor Clara, that really got me, right here." He nodded sadly. "I don't believe I've ever seen a man so torn up over a woman."

Clara turned and looked at the salesman. Could he be talking about Emmett?

"Excuse me," she asked politely, "but was this man tall, with big brown puppy-dog eyes and beautiful silvery flowing hair?"

The salesman nodded enthusiastically. "You know him?"

She nodded in return. "I'm Clara—"

The salesman raised his eyebrows in surprise. "Well, Clara," he said with a sincerity only a salesman could muster, "if you have any feelings toward him whatsoever, go find him. I've never seen a man more tore up or in love than he was, and love like that doesn't happen too often. Whatever happened between you two, I'd give him a second chance."

Clara stared at the salesman for a second. She realized he was right.

She stood and pulled the emergency cord.

"Emmett!" she whispered.

Iron wheels screamed as the train jerked to a stop. Clara hurried down the aisle, ignoring the shouts of passengers and the questions of the conductors. She quickly descended the steps and began the walk back into town.

Maybe, she thought, it had been her own stubborn pride that made her want to run away from Doc. Well, she was a stubborn woman—more than one man had told her so. Only this time, she was going to use that stubbornness to find and keep the man she loved!

Marty heard Tannen's voice, calling from out in the street: "All right, runt, time's up!"

He looked out the window. He guessed he was as ready as he would ever be. The two gunslingers still held Doc, but Tannen was staring in toward the shop where Marty stood. And there was another change, too. In the minute Marty had taken to get ready for their confrontation, all the doors and windows on the other side of the street had filled with onlookers—the citizens of Hill Valley were going to get their show after all.

Marty checked out his outfit in the mirror at the back of the store. It was all in place—the hat, the sarapé, the gunbelt—just like Clint Eastwood in *A Fistful of Dollars*. Now, all he had to do was act like Clint Eastwood.

"I've got a bullet here for you, Eastwood!" Buford screamed. "Aimed right for your heart!"

That was just what Marty wanted. He stepped out onto the street. "I'm right here, Tannen."

Mad Dog Tannen grinned. "Draw!" he demanded.

Instead, Marty unbuckled his gunbelt and let it fall to the ground. "No," he said, slowly and confidently, "I thought we could settle this thing like *men*."

Tannen's grin got even wider. "You thought wrong, dude." He drew his pistol and fired.

Marty fell to the ground.

Buford Tannen laughed and sauntered over to his fallen foe.

Marty opened his eyes and kicked the gun from Tannen's hand! Tannen's jaw dropped as the gun went flying across the street.

Marty jumped to his feet.

Tannen rushed him, aiming a fist straight for his gut. He howled in pain as his knuckles smashed against something solid.

Marty threw back his sarapé to reveal the cast-iron door he had taken off the potbellied stove. Now that it had served its purpose, he could unstrap this thing from his chest.

"It's broke!" Buford wailed, holding up his nerveless hand for all to see. "My gun hand's broke, dammit!" He looked up at Marty and growled, grabbing for the teenager with the hand he had left.

Marty grabbed the stove door and smashed it on top of Tannen's head. The blow sent Buford reeling sideways.

Marty threw the door down. The rest of this fight was going to be settled with fists.

Mad Dog Tannen shook his head and blinked, then rushed Marty one more time.

Marty socked his opponent square in the face, sending him tumbling backward over a hitching rail. But you couldn't keep a Mad Dog down. Tannen staggered to his feet again and rushed Marty, hitting the teen with his right hand.

Tannen had forgotten what happened to his right hand. He screamed in pain. He swung at Marty with his left, but Marty easily sidestepped the blow. This was getting pitiful. Marty gave Tannen a good hearty shove.

Buford Tannen fell into the tombstone—the same tombstone in the photo—breaking the stone in half! Somehow, he got to his feet again, but he couldn't really stand anymore. Instead, he stumbled backward, into a cart Marty had seen when he'd first come to town—a cart filled with damp, fragrant manure!

Buford passed out, covered in brown.

Marty turned to study the three members of Tannen's gang. The three outlaws exchanged a look, and then, without a word, let go of Doc and started to run. They were followed quickly by three sheriff's deputies.

Marty walked over to his friend. "You okay, Doc?"

"I'm fine, Marty." Doc brushed his coat where the gunmen had held him.

A young boy, maybe seven or eight, ran across the street to get a better look.

"Wow!" the boy shouted excitedly. "Armor! How'd you think of that, mister?"

Marty shrugged. "I saw it in a Clint Eastwood movie."

The boy frowned. "Movie? What's a movie?"

Oh, that was right. In the thrill of victory, Marty had forgotten where he was. Still, as he recalled from his high school film history course, movies should be showing up pretty soon.

"You'll find out," he told the boy with a smile.

The other townspeople started to gather around as well. One of them shooed the boy away:

"Move along, D.W., move along."

Another fellow, wearing what looked like a barber's smock, shook his head. "That little Griffith boy, can't hold him down."

Marty frowned, remembering his film history course all over again. Griffith boy? D.W.? Naww.

All thoughts of history left his head as he saw another of the local deputies move quickly over to the semiconscious outlaw. The deputy drew his gun. "Buford Tannen, you're under arrest for the murder of Marshal James Strickland."

Tannen raised his hands and tried to stand.

In the distance, the train whistle blew. Marty

looked over at Doc. That had to mean the train was leaving the station.

"Can we make it?" Marty asked.

Doc considered the question for a second before nodding. "We'll have to cut 'em off at Coyote Pass!"

Doc grabbed his horse and untied a second one for Marty—the second animal looked an awful lot like the one Buford rode. They both mounted up.

There, in the middle of the crowd, Marty saw Seamus McFly. Marty picked up his gunbelt and waved at his great-great-grandfather. "Seamus! Here!" He threw the belt over to the farmer. "Trade it in on a new hat!"

"Thank you, Mr. Eastwood!" Seamus replied as he deftly caught the gift.

Marty looked over his shoulder as he turned his horse to go. "And take care of that baby!"

Doc and Marty took off at a full gallop.

Clara had made it to town at last! There was a crowd in front of the Palace Saloon. Clara ran toward them as she saw a pair of deputies lead a very dirty and disoriented Buford Tannen across the street toward the jailhouse. It looked like something serious had happened here.

She also had seen a pair of riders gallop around the corner as she approached. They were too far away for Clara to tell for sure, but one of them looked as if he had a long mane of silver hair.

"Emmett?" she called.

But there was no reply.

She ran down the street to the blacksmith shop and flung open the doors, her momentum carrying her halfway into the barn.

"Emmett!" she called again. "Emmett!"

The shop appeared to be empty. Even the horses were gone. Perhaps it was Emmett she had seen, riding away with young Clint. But where?

She spotted a tabletop model of some sort pushed up against one of the walls. It was partially covered by canvas, but once she pulled the covering off, she realized it was a tiny reproduction of Hill Valley, much like the map she had seen in the waiting room of the train depot, with Main Street, the courthouse tower, the Palace Saloon, even the train station. And running from the train station was a set of miniature tracks, with a point at the far end of the tracks marked STOP TRAIN HERE—a point that, if she understood this model reconstruction, was very near the ravine where Emmett had saved her!

"Stop train here"? Was this the mystery that Emmett wouldn't tell her about? Why would they want to stop a train?

Well, Clara decided, she was about to find out. She had seen Clint's horse tied up in front of the barn. She was sure he wouldn't mind if she borrowed it, especially for something as important as this.

No matter what was happening, Clara swore this: She would not be left behind!

•Chapter Nineteen•

Marty could see it below—a thick black smudge moving along a thin black line. It was the train, just entering Coyote Pass, and by urging their horses over Gale Ridge, they were ahead of it! Now, if they could just keep their horses at a gallop down the steep hill that led into the pass, they had a chance to overtake the train before it passed by the spur with the DeLorean.

Doc whooped as he started Archimedes down the hill. Marty's horse leapt after Doc's lead, and a moment later, they were galloping full-speed across level ground to intercept the train. Marty's horse pulled ahead, as if the stallion knew exactly what was expected of it and was eager for the rendezvous. It occurred to Marty that if this was indeed Mad Dog Tannen's horse, it probably would be very experienced in this sort of thing.

But the train had reached the level ground as well, and it was gaining speed. Marty and Doc both managed to pull their horses parallel to the last passenger car, but their mounts couldn't stand this pace for much longer. Doc reached over and grabbed the ladder on the side of the car, pulling himself off his horse. After steadying himself and taking a deep breath, Doc climbed to the roof of the car as Archimedes fell behind, and Marty pulled his steed alongside the car and pulled himself up the ladder as well.

Once he was sure that Marty was safely on board, Doc led the way forward, running across the tops of the cars toward the locomotive. Doc stopped, though, before they reached the tender— that car behind the engine where they kept all the coal. Doc raised his hand—the signal, Marty realized—and they both covered their lower faces with their bandannas. They climbed forward over the covered half of the tender, until Marty could see into the cab at the rear of the locomotive. As they had expected, there were two men down below, the engineer and the fireman, both of them facing toward the front of the engine.

Doc drew one of the guns he had stored in Archimedes's saddlebag and jumped down behind the engineer.

"Do what I say and you won't get hurt," Doc said in his most threatening voice (which, Marty had to admit, didn't sound very threatening).

The engineer put up his hands anyway. Marty climbed down into the back of the cab to cover the fireman.

"Is this a holdup?" the engineer asked in a quavering voice.

Doc shook his head. "It's a science experiment." He waved his gun toward the front of the train. "Stop the train just before you hit that switchtrack up ahead."

The engineer did as Doc said, throwing on the brake so that the train squealed to a halt less than ten feet from the point where the track divided.

"Marty, throw the switch," Doc ordered, then waved his gun at the fireman. "You, uncouple the cars from the tender."

Both Marty and the fireman jumped from the cab. Marty ran forward to the long wooden pole that served as a switching mechanism. He put his back into it and yanked the track over so that the locomotive would head for the ravine. As Marty ran back to the train, he saw that the fireman had uncoupled the cars as he had been ordered.

Doc was staring at the engineer as Marty approached. After a moment's pause, Doc pulled off the engineer's cap, then handed the railroad man his own broad-brimmed, black hat.

"You can get off now," Doc remarked as he put the engineer's cap on his head.

The engineer dutifully jumped off. Marty climbed back into the cab as Doc started the locomotive, and they slowly pulled away from the rest of the train.

Clara urged her horse through the trees. They had been climbing for some time now. She wasn't quite sure where they were, but by keeping the sun more or less in front of her horse as she rode, she should be headed in the general direction of the ravine.

The forest ended, and she found herself on a bluff overlooking what must be Coyote Pass. There, below her, was what at first she took to be the train, stopped halfway down the valley, until she realized that the train's engine was missing.

Emmett and Clint must have been here already and taken the locomotive. But why would Emmett want to steal a locomotive?

Clara spurred her horse into a gallop, riding along the ridge parallel to the tracks. She had missed them in the pass, but she might still be able to head them off on the other side. She would find out, if it was the last thing she did in Hill Valley, exactly what Emmett L. Brown was up to.

They had driven the locomotive fairly slowly for the half mile or so until they reached the DeLorean. They wanted to conserve as much fuel as possible for their final run at the ravine. But Doc, apparently, didn't want to depend on wood alone. As soon as he had stopped the locomotive, he instructed Marty to climb down and hand the inventor three cylindrical, cloth-covered packages that Doc had stashed in the DeLorean the day before. Marty picked up the first of the three, wrapped in green cloth with a big number 1 printed on it. It was about a foot and a half long and nine inches around, and was surprisingly heavy for so small a package.

Marty passed the green package up to Doc, then retrieved the second, yellow-covered cylinder. He gave that to Doc in turn, then picked up the last of the three, wrapped in red.

"What are these things, anyway?" Marty asked as he passed this one, too, to Doc.

"My own version of Presto Logs," the inventor replied as he stacked the red cylinder next to the other two in a corner of the cab. "Compressed wood with anthracite dust, chemically treated to burn hotter and longer. I use 'em in my forge so I don't have to stoke it." He pointed at the large number 3 on the red log. "These three in the furnace will ignite sequentially, make the fire burn hotter, kick up the boiler pressure, and make the train go faster."

Marty nodded. There was nobody else like Doc. Maybe this new plan of his would actually get the locomotive, and the DeLorean, up to eighty-eight, and they could get out of here before they crashed into the ravine.

Doc waved as Marty walked over to the De-Lorean. Marty opened the car door and climbed down behind the wheel. The walkie-talkie—the same one they had used to rescue the sports book from Biff—sat on the passenger seat.

"Testing, Marty!" Doc's voice crackled through the walkie-talkie's tiny speaker. Marty picked up the two-way radio and extended the antenna. He pushed a button on the radio's side.

"That's a big ten-four," he replied.

"Then let's go home," Doc's voice replied.

Marty released the emergency brake and shifted the car into neutral.

"Ready to roll!" he said into the walkie-talkie.

He looked in the rearview mirror as Doc tooted the train whistle. Marty could hear air hiss heavily from the cylinders behind the wheels as Doc released the locomotive's brakes. And then the pistons started to push the wheels as Doc opened the throttle. The engine eased forward.

Marty tried to keep from tensing as the locomotive rolled forward to the back of the DeLorean. Now, if the cowcatcher would just grab the back bumper of the car, and push it forward— Doc had assured Marty that the locomotive would not smash through the DeLorean, but still, Doc had been wrong before.

Marty was jolted forward. He heard a crunch as the cowcatcher hit the bumper. He grabbed for the door handle, but stopped when he realized the DeLorean was moving. The locomotive was pushing the car forward!

Marty grinned. They were on their way!

Clara had reached the tracks at last. Letting her memory of the tabletop model in the blacksmith's shop guide her, she had headed for the branch line that ran to the ravine, and she had guessed correctly. There, only a few hundred feet ahead, was the locomotive, slowly pulling away. She was close enough to see what she thought was the back of Emmett's head, although he no longer wore his wide-brimmed, black hat, his silver hair now falling from below a striped engineer's cap.

"Emmett!" she called.

The train kept moving. Emmett couldn't hear her over the locomotive engine.

But she was too close to stop now. She kept her horse at a gallop. She was almost there. As long as the locomotive didn't gain speed too quickly, she could overtake them in no time at all.

Clara leaned forward, kicking her mount's flanks, urging it to greater speed.

She was almost to her Emmett.

Great Scott!

Doc pulled the cord that blew the whistle. He had never realized, until now, how enjoyable it would be to run a locomotive.

Of course, Doc reminded himself, enjoyment was surely secondary in the present situation, considering the finite amount of track they had before them and the velocity they had to reach. It was time, quite frankly, to get down to business.

Doc thumbed the talk switch on his two-way radio. "Marty, are the time circuits on?"

There was a moment's pause, followed by Marty's voice: "Check, Doc."

"Input the destination time," Doc instructed. "October 17, 1985. Eleven A.M."

"Check!" Marty's voice crackled back on the walkie-talkie.

Doc picked up the green-wrapped cylinder. "I'm

throwing in the Presto Logs," he announced to the walkie-talkie. "Once they get going, we'll *really* get going!"

Doc took a deep breath and threw the first of the three logs into the boiler. There was no turning back, no matter what he felt. For his sake, for Marty's sake, for the sake of the space-time continuum, it was time to go back to the future.

The train was gaining speed, but Clara's horse was faster still. They were closing in on the tender.

At a moment like this, she was certainly glad she had led an active childhood back in her native New Jersey. True, she hadn't ridden a horse or done any serious climbing for years, but those were the sort of things you never forgot.

There was a ladder on the back of the tender. She had to pull her horse next to the ladder, grab onto one of the rungs, and pull herself off her horse and onto the moving train. Not a simple thing to do, but if both horse and train were traveling at the same constant speed, with no jarring distractions, she should be able to accomplish it easily.

She pulled the horse parallel to the ladder. She had to do it, for her future with Emmett!

Marty looked down at the speedometer on the DeLorean.

"We're running steady at twenty-five miles an hour," he announced. Not anywhere near as fast as they needed to go, he thought, but didn't say aloud.

Doc's voice called reassuringly over the walkie-talkie. "The first log should fire any moment now."

So this was it, Marty thought. If the effects were going to be anywhere near as spectacular as Doc had described, as soon as that log caught fire, he would have to brace himself for the shock. But if the locomotive didn't explode, or lurch forward so violently that it pushed the DeLorean off the tracks, they should really be able to get some speed!

Clara reached over and firmly grasped the bottom rung of the ladder.

The world exploded around her. There was a great booming roar, and the air above the locomotive was filled with green smoke and flame. With a terrible suddenness, the car jerked forward, pulling her from her horse!

She managed to grab the ladder with her other hand as well, before the wind hit her, almost tearing her from her perch. The locomotive was traveling at a fantastic speed, and she could barely manage to hang on, her shoes mere inches from the ground and certain injury!

"Emmett!" she called with all the strength in her.

But the locomotive's engine was roaring now. There was no way anybody could hear or help. And with every passing second, it felt as if they were going faster still!

•Chapter Twenty•

Marty grinned. This was more like it. The De-
Lorean's speedometer was climbing steadily—
36—37—38.

"I'm coming aboard!" Doc's voice shouted on
the walkie-talkie.

Marty reached across the DeLorean and opened
the gull-wing door on the passenger side. He
looked in the rearview mirror and saw Doc climb
forward out of the cab onto a narrow walkway on
the side of the engine.

So far, so good. Marty looked ahead, but still
couldn't see the windmill—their fail-safe point.
Everything was moving on schedule—so far.

Why did he always feel like something was going to go wrong?

• • •

She had had to call upon reserves of strength she didn't even know she possessed, but Clara had pulled herself up the ladder, rung after rung, fighting the wind and the ever-increasing vibration. It was more than the fear of injury that had driven her. She felt very strongly—so strongly that it surprised her—that finding Emmett was the most important thing she might ever do. Not only was he the man for her, although she didn't always believe so strongly in those romantic notions. No, there was something very different about that man, as if he came from a different place—a place that Clara felt she could also belong in a way she never had back in New Jersey.

Her commitment gave her strength, and her strength allowed her to climb up the ladder to the top of the tender. She looked down at the pile of logs below, then to the cab beyond.

The cab was deserted. Emmett was no longer there! She looked beyond the cab and saw him climbing along the side of the engine, toward a strange-looking silver carriage that was running in front of the locomotive. Why would there be a carriage in front of the locomotive? She realized with every passing moment, she had less idea what her man was doing. But she was sure that, no matter what, once they could talk again, everything would be resolved.

"Emmett!" she called, but he was still too far ahead to hear. Well, she would just have to go a little farther to get him, then. She climbed down gingerly onto the woodpile.

Then the world exploded again, and she was falling.

Great Scott!

The yellow log ignited, sending yellow smoke and flame high in the air. And the vibration almost knocked Doc completely off the side of the locomotive! If he hadn't grabbed a handhold at the last possible second, he would have fallen from the locomotive, and considering the speed they had now attained, he could have risked serious injury—or worse!

Doc paused a moment to control his breathing. The train was going so fast now that the countryside had become a blur, and the train shook as it bounced over the track. He had to be more careful. Even with all that work they'd done rejuvenating him in the future, he still wasn't as young as he used to be.

He silently swore to concentrate, to let *nothing* distract him, and headed once more for the DeLorean.

Marty had worried there for a moment when the second log had erupted. The force of the explosion had been even greater than the first, but when he had checked the rearview mirror, he saw Doc was hanging on to a handhold on the side of the locomotive. The inventor must have actually estimated the time of the explosion and used the handhold to ensure against a possible accident. Obviously, Doc had everything under control.

The speedometer had passed forty-five, and was

climbing quickly to fifty. Marty didn't know why he had doubted anything. They were really going to do it!

The woodpile had fallen with Clara, cushioning her fall. She might have a bruise or two when this was all over, but, Lord willing, she hadn't broken anything. She climbed off the end of the woodpile and into the cab of the locomotive, and once again called Emmett's name.

He still couldn't hear her. It was simply too noisy. She stuck her head around the side of the cab and waved, but Emmett was facing away, using all his concentration to move to the front of the locomotive. She stuck her entire upper body out of the side of the cab and screamed for all she was worth while waving both her arms. There was still no reaction. Emmett was too intent on climbing down on the cowcatcher to pay attention to anything as small as a human voice.

But what else, Clara wondered, could she use to get his attention?

Great Scott!

Doc stopped halfway down the cowcatcher. He had just heard the train whistle blow. And that meant there had to be somebody in the locomotive cab who could make that whistle blow.

His mouth fell open as he turned back to the cab. "Clara!" he called.

"Emmett!" his beloved called back. "I love you!"

Great Scott!

• • •

The DeLorean was about to hit fifty-five. But where was Doc? Marty looked out the rearview mirror and saw the inventor on the cowcatcher, looking back at the locomotive.

"Yo, Doc," Marty called into his radio, "what's happening?"

"It's Clara!" Doc's voice barked back. "She's on the train!"

Clara? *The schoolteacher?* On the train? "That's impossible!" Marty called back.

"She's here!" Doc insisted. "In the cab! I've got to go back for her!"

Marty saw Doc climb back up to the top of the cowcatcher.

"What are you gonna do?" Marty asked.

"Hope there's enough time to stop the train," Doc's voice crackled back, "and get her off before we hit the bridge!"

Marty looked out the front windshield. There, on the left, coming up fast, was the windmill, their fail-safe point! Once they were past the windmill, there wouldn't be enough time to stop the train before they reached the ravine.

"Doc!" Marty shouted into the radio. "I see the windmill!" He glanced down at the speedometer. "And we're going sixty! You'll never make it!"

As Marty finished the sentence, he saw the windmill go past.

Now there was no way to stop the train before it plunged into the ravine.

• • •

It only took Doc a second to make the decision. A part of him had wanted him to make this decision all along.

"Then we'll have to take her with us!" he shouted into the walkie-talkie. "Keep calling out the speed!" He tucked the radio back into his coat pocket and reached out his free hand to his beloved.

"Clara!" he called. "Climb out here to me!"

But the schoolteacher looked doubtful. "I don't know if I can."

"You can do it!" Doc shouted back enthusiastically. "Just don't look down!"

Clara took a deep breath and climbed from the cab onto the walkway.

"Sixty-five miles an hour!" Marty's voice called over the radio.

Doc waved Clara forward. "Good! You're doing fine! Nice and steady!"

Clara smiled uncertainly as she eased her feet along the narrow walkway.

"Keep coming," Doc encouraged.

"Seventy!" Marty's voice announced from Doc's pocket.

Great Scott! They were going so fast now, a fall from the locomotive would certainly mean death. Still, Doc couldn't think of such a thing. Clara was a surefooted woman, and there were only a few feet left between them.

The third log exploded with a roar.

Clara screamed as she was thrown from the walkway.

•Chapter Twenty-One•

As Clara fell, she saw the sky full of smoke the color of blood.

Her back banged painfully against the side of the locomotive as she swung down. But then she stopped. She realized there was a different, painful pressure on her left leg, like it was wedged against something. Her leg must have gotten caught between the engine and the walkway and kept her from falling farther.

She looked beneath her and wished she hadn't. The ground rushed by less than a yard away, but—far worse than that—the pounding piston wheels were inches from her head!

"Help!" she called.

From somewhere, she heard Clint Eastwood's voice shout, "Seventy-five!"

She tried to lift her head, to see if there was

someplace on the locomotive where she could get a handhold, but the wind rushing by the speeding train pushed her back.

"Emmett!" she yelled. "Help!"

If Emmett said anything in return, it was lost in the wind.

Marty could see it all in the rearview mirror. Both Doc and Clara had slipped when the third log had exploded, falling down the side of the locomotive. Doc had managed to grab a handhold on the side of the train, but Clara's leg had become wedged in some sort of metal brace along the walkway. That was the only thing still holding her on the train. If her leg somehow slipped, she would go crashing down, right into the wheels.

Doc glanced over at the schoolteacher, trying to figure out some way to grab Clara without falling off the locomotive himself. But they were going far too fast now. With the rushing air and the way the locomotive was jumping on the uneven tracks, Doc was having trouble just hanging on.

Marty looked forward to check their speed. The digital readout read eighty miles an hour.

"Eighty," Marty said into the walkie-talkie, and then realized, ahead of him, he could already see the half-completed bridge over the ravine. That meant there were only seconds left before the locomotive would go crashing over the edge— seconds before both Doc and Clara would die.

There had to be something Marty could do! Here he was, in a car from a hundred years in the future. Wasn't there something about this car, or something that Marty had learned in his travels through time, that could save his friends?

He glanced down at the speedometer. It was up to eighty-three. It looked like Doc's special Presto Logs might actually work. But how could Marty face 1985 again, if he knew Doc had died to get him there?

Think! Marty told himself.

And then he remembered.

Ahead of them, Doc could see the ravine.

"Eighty!" Marty's voice announced on the walkie-talkie. He turned back to Clara.

"I'm slipping!" the schoolteacher screamed. Doc saw that her leg was, indeed, working its way out of the brace. He would have to grab for her, somehow, even if it pulled him off of the locomotive, too.

"Doc!" Marty's voice called over the walkie-talkie. "Here! Catch!"

Catch? Doc turned back to the DeLorean. Marty had opened his gull-wing door and was leaning out, the pink hoverboard in his hand.

The hoverboard! Great Scott! That was the very reason why Doc always brought everything with him when time traveling. You never knew the precise tools you were going to need.

Marty tossed the hoverboard straight for Doc's feet! Doc snagged it with his left foot then, balancing himself precariously on the pink, floating piece of wood, moved himself hand over hand along the locomotive toward Clara. So far, so good. But that ravine was coming up awfully fast. Doc stared at the pink board now in his hands. How exactly did you use one of these things, anyway?

Clara was sure that death was near. Her leg was slipping free of wherever it had jammed, and she imagined she could feel the pistons and wheels beneath her, brushing against her hair. For some reason, she felt oddly calm. A few days before, Emmett had saved her as her wagon was about to plunge into a ravine. Now, though, she would die after all, when she had tried to talk to Emmett again, on a speeding locomotive headed for that very same ravine. It was enough to make one believe in fate. Maybe, Clara thought, there were some things that couldn't be changed.

She felt two strong hands grab her wrists. She looked up to see Emmett standing next to her and smiling.

Wait a moment. This train was going at an incredible rate of speed. How could Emmett be standing beside her?

Emmett pulled her to him, away from the wildly spinning wheels, as her leg came free from whatever held it. She saw, as he pulled her to him, that he was standing on some sort of oval board, painted a very bright pink, and, furthermore, that that board was just hanging in the air!

Clara thought briefly of Jules Verne. Could there have been some truth in what Emmett had told her? But then Emmett hugged her to him, and she embraced him as well.

There were new explosions—this time, from that strange, silver railroad car in front of the locomotive—three explosions, and three flashes of light. And then, that strange car vanished from the tracks—just completely disappeared except for two trails of flame! But the locomotive, still beside them, roared onward, through a barrier erected across the half-built bridge, over the end of the tracks and down into the ravine. There was an explosion greater than any Clara had heard before as the locomotive hit the rocks below.

She closed her eyes, waiting for the strange board that held Emmett and herself to follow the train. At least, she thought, they could die together!

But the board had stopped moving. Clara opened her eyes and saw that they floated near the edge of the ravine, but still over solid ground. She looked into Emmett's eyes. It was so good to see him again!

They kissed. Oh, how could they have ever quarreled? How could they ever be parted? But they held each other now. That was all that mattered. Now, they would have time for everything.

Emmett shifted his weight and kicked the ground beneath the floating board. Still holding each other tightly, the two of them flew, together, off into the western sky.

•Chapter Twenty-Two•

October 17, 1985, 11 A.M.

Marty saw Doc save Clara with the hoverboard. He breathed a sigh of relief as he looked back at the instrument panel of the DeLorean.

The speedometer read eighty-eight miles per hour.

There were three sonic booms, and three flashes of brilliant light. And the DeLorean was traveling across the bridge. Except now the bridge was whole. Marty glanced down at the digital display and saw that the current year was 1985. He was home.

The DeLorean coasted onto solid ground on the far end of the bridge, the friction of the metal railroad wheels slowing the car now that there was no longer a locomotive pushing from behind. Marty was surprised how relieved he was to see the good old world of Hill Valley—his Hill Valley—one more time. The car was passing the cliff road, now. Wait a minute! The historic Clayton Ravine sign had changed. The new sign said it was called the Eastwood Ravine now—Marty winced—named after some big locomotive wreck in 1885. The DeLorean was moving too fast for him to read any more, but that was enough. He just hoped his time traveling hadn't changed anything else in 1985.

He was happy to be home, though, and glad that Doc had rescued Clara with the hoverboard. Still, he was sad underneath it all, and maybe a little angry, too. After all both Marty and Doc had been through, when they had been so close to success, Doc had had to stay behind!

At least Doc was probably safe back there now, what with Mad Dog Tannen arrested and all. Marty wondered, though, if he should consider taking the DeLorean back there one more time to pick up his friend. If only he knew what the inventor wanted! Maybe, Marty hoped, Doc would send him another letter.

The car was coasting by the Hilldale housing development now, the place where the railroad tracks crossed the main highway. He could hear the crossing gates clanging up ahead as the barriers lowered to stop traffic. Hey! It was pretty neat the way those gates closed when even something as small as the DeLorean showed up on the tracks.

Marty heard a low, moaning sound—not an old-fashioned train whistle, but a modern diesel horn.

Maybe, he realized, the crossing gates wouldn't

close for something as small as a DeLorean. He looked down the tracks as the car swung around a shallow curve. There, directly ahead of him, was a diesel engine headed his way. With the train wheels on the DeLorean locked on the tracks, there was no way he could turn to avoid a head-on collision!

The DeLorean had almost slowed to a complete stop by now, but the diesel showed no sign of changing speed. Marty threw open the gull-wing door. He jumped and rolled clear.

He stopped himself and looked up to see the diesel engine smash into the DeLorean at sixty miles an hour or better.

The DeLorean was totaled. Bits and pieces of the time machine were sent flying everywhere. Marty ducked and covered his head with his arms to protect himself from the flying debris.

The diesel didn't even stop. It just kept on going, as if the engineer hadn't even noticed the DeLorean was there.

Marty uncovered his head and stood as the train sped away.

"Oh, God, no!" Marty cried. "No!"

There were twisted bits of the DeLorean everywhere. There was no way to get Doc now—not anymore. Marty fell to his knees. After all that had happened, this was just too much to take.

"Well, Doc," he said, once he'd gotten control of himself. "It's destroyed. Just like you wanted."

Marty stood at last. There was no reason for him to stay. It was time to go the rest of the way home.

• • •

Marty trudged through the entrance to the Lyon Estates. He should be happy to see his parents, his house, his brother and sister, but somehow, there didn't seem to be any rush to get home, now that he would never see Doc again.

He walked up the winding street, reaching his own driveway at last. Biff was outside, waxing Marty's father's BMW. The garage door was open, and Marty could see his black Toyota Four-By-Four inside. All in all, things looked pretty much the way he had left them. As far as Marty could tell, there were no more surprises like that Eastwood Ravine.

Biff waved as he walked up the drive.

"Hiya, Marty!" Biff called. "Gone cowboy, eh?"

Marty glanced down at his clothes. He was still wearing the western clothes he had used to face Mad Dog Tannen—sarapé, boots and all.

"Yeah," he answered without much enthusiasm. He glanced over at the job the other Tannen was doing on the BMW. "Uh, Biff, two coats of wax, right?"

"Yep," Biff agreed amiably. "Puttin' on the second coat right now." He grabbed his cloth and got back to work.

Marty turned up the sidewalk and walked toward the front door. His brother, Dave, dressed in a suit and tie, walked out of the house as Marty approached the steps.

"Marty!" Dave grinned as he straightened his tie. "When did you—" He paused and frowned as he took a better look at his brother. "Hey, who are you supposed to be? Clint Eastwood?"

Marty nodded. "Yeah," he replied. His brother had pegged him exactly.

"He's gone cowboy," Biff explained, looking up from his waxing.

Dave grinned at that all over again. "So, Marty, when did you get back?"

Marty stared at his brother. Dave had said those same words to him before—in another time, another world, really—that other 1985, when Biff had stolen the sports almanac and controlled all of Hill Valley. Marty almost shivered. When you traveled through time, déjà vu could get really strange.

But he really didn't know what his brother was talking about. That was another problem with time travel—it could get real confusing.

"Back?" Marty asked. "Back from where, Dave?"

"I thought you and Jennifer went up to the lake," his brother explained.

Of course! It all came back to Marty. That's what Jennifer and he were about to do that morning, when Doc had shown up from the future.

Jennifer?

"Jennifer!" Marty yelled. "Oh, my God, Jennifer!"

With the accident with the DeLorean and all that stuff in the past, he had forgotten completely about his girl friend. He ran inside the house and grabbed the keys to his truck. His mother and father both called to him as he hurried past. Maybe it was his rush, or maybe it was his cowboy clothes, but both of them looked worried as they came to the front door, followed by Dave and Lorraine. Marty's whole family watched him back his Four-By-Four out into the street.

Marty drove to Jennifer's house as quickly as he dared.

He remembered how he and Doc had left her, back in that other 1985, thinking that she would be safe. They didn't realize, then, that the world had changed because of what Biff had done with the sports almanac. By the time they had figured out she might have been in danger, it was too late to go back for her, although Doc had assured Marty that Jennifer would be fine. As long as they got the book back from Biff, the world would be the one Marty remembered, and not the twisted future Biff had created. And they had gotten the book, so everything was fine, now—right? So what was he worried about?

As much as Marty hated to admit it, sometimes even Doc could be wrong.

Marty pulled into Jennifer's driveway. Her house looked fine—no bars on the windows or any of the other stuff from that bad 1985. And there was the hammock, the same place they'd left Jennifer in that other world.

Marty jumped from the car and ran to the hammock. There, still asleep, was the girl he loved.

"Thank God!" He shook her gently. "Jen?" he called gently. "Jennifer?"

She moaned softly in her sleep—a deep, exhausted sleep, like she'd been through a lot.

Marty realized she had, they all had. But Marty needed her to wake up. He had to talk to her, to make sure she was all right, and, he guessed, to reassure himself that he was finally back in the real 1985.

He leaned down and kissed her.

She opened her eyes with a start, but when she saw him, she smiled.

"Marty!" She reached her arms up to hug him. "I had a terrible nightmare."

"Yeah," Marty agreed. "Me, too." A nightmare, he thought, that was over at last.

Jennifer frowned as she looked at his hat. "Marty, what are you wearing?"

Marty shrugged. "I've gone cowboy."

Jennifer felt like she had been asleep for years. She had gotten out of the hammock after Marty had woken her, and agreed when he suggested they take his truck for a drive. She thought that moving around, with the fresh air blowing in her face, would wake her the rest of the way, but even that wasn't working today.

"Marty, what's going on?" she asked, shaking her head sharply. "I feel so out of it, like I don't know what day it is."

Marty sighed. "I know the feeling."

That wasn't quite it, though—not waking up. It was more like she wasn't sure when she'd been awake and when she'd been asleep. She tried to explain: "But this is more like, well, like something happened that I can't quite remember . . ."

It was almost like she had been living in a

dream. But how could she say that to Marty and make any sense?

She gasped. There, outside the window, was her dream.

"What?" Marty asked her. "What's wrong?"

She put her hand on Marty's shoulder. "Stop the truck."

Marty did as she asked. They were outside the Hilldale housing development. It wasn't finished yet. Only a few of the units were standing, and those were all covered with multicolored pennants and GRAND OPENING signs.

But Jennifer remembered another Hilldale from her dream—an older Hilldale, the whole place sort of run-down and falling apart, a Hilldale where she was living with Marty—and their kids, they had had two of them, a boy and a girl—in the future?

"Hilldale," Marty said appreciatively. "You know, this might be a pretty good place to live, huh?"

Jennifer shivered. She remembered that dream all too well, about how Marty had given up on life. And what had happened to her?

"No," she replied firmly.

Marty looked over at her, surprised. "I meant—in the future."

Jennifer shook her head. The dream was all flooding back now, and it wasn't the way she wanted to live her life. "I never want to live here. Ever."

Marty grinned sheepishly. "Hey, okay, sorry. I just thought—"

She looked away from the development, trying to drive the dream from her head. "Marty, could we just drive away from here, please?"

Marty shifted the car into first.

"Jennifer, what's wrong?" he asked as they started to move.

She sighed. "My dream, it was so real. About the future—about us—about our kids. Our kids were a mess, and you were, I don't know, you had some weird job working for Needles."

Marty frowned. "Needles? From school? He has a job?"

"Yeah," she answered, "and you got fired. It was terrible."

"What?" Marty stopped the truck at a traffic light. He turned to look at her. "Wait a minute. I got *fired*?"

He was getting awfully upset about this, like he knew something about the dream, too. Was there something he wasn't telling her?

"Marty," Jennifer asked, "it *was* just a dream, wasn't it?"

Before Marty could answer, a souped-up red racing truck pulled up next to them. The driver gunned the engine. Jennifer looked over and saw the truck was full of guys from their high school.

"Hey, the big M!" the guy in the driver's seat yelled. "How's it hangin', McFly?"

"Needles!" Marty called.

Jennifer looked closer and saw Needles behind the wheel—only now he was seventeen years old, not middle-aged like he had been in the dream from the future. Jennifer frowned. He was supposed to be seventeen years old, wasn't he? They were all seniors in high school, weren't they? Then why did she keep seeing everybody the way they were in the dream?

Needles raced his engine again. "Nice wheels, McFly. Let's see what she can do."

Marty waved away the offer. "No thanks, Needles." He pulled his truck forward a few feet so the two vehicles were no longer lined up.

"C'mon, McFly," Needles yelled. "What's the matter—chicken?"

Marty frowned as the other guys in Needles's truck made clucking noises. His hands turned white where they gripped the wheel.

Oh, no, Jennifer thought. She had been through this chicken business before. This stubborn streak was the one thing she didn't like about Marty.

Marty backed up the truck. He glared at Needles. "Nobody calls me chicken!"

Marty raced his engine. Needles hit his accelerator, too.

Jennifer felt there was something terribly wrong here. She grabbed her boyfriend's elbow. "Marty. Don't—"

There was more to it, she realized, than Marty being stubborn. Doc had talked to her in that all-too-real dream, told her something about Marty having an accident with his Four-By-Four, about how that accident changed his whole life, for the worse.

And now it looked like that dream accident was going to take place in real life.

Marty put his hand on the stick shift. He looked up at the stoplight. Jennifer saw the light for traffic going the other way had turned from green to yellow. Needles gunned his engine again, and Marty pressed his foot down on the clutch.

Jennifer opened her mouth, but she didn't know what to say. Wasn't there any way she could stop this from happening? And all because of this "Nobody calls me chicken!" business.

The light turned green. Needles's racing truck roared away from the intersection.

Marty just sat there. He turned to Jennifer, shrugged, and smiled.

"And he's definitely nobody," Marty said.

Jennifer smiled back. Maybe, somewhere, somehow, Marty had learned something about himself, and how there might be different ways to prove who you were. She liked this Marty McFly. He was the kind of fellow she could really have a future with.

A horn blared up ahead, followed by a squeal of brakes. They both looked out the windshield as Needles's truck swerved, barely missing a Rolls Royce that had started out a side street.

"Jeez!" Marty yelled. "I would have hit that Rolls Royce!"

"Rolls Royce?" Jennifer repeated. That was exactly what Doc Brown had told her in the dream—Marty was supposed to have the accident with a Rolls Royce.

This *was* more than just a dream. There was a piece of paper in her pocket, a paper she remembered.

She pulled out the crumpled page and looked at the huge letters at the center: YOU'RE FIRED.

There! It wasn't a dream after all! It was—

The words disappeared from the page.

"It erased!" she exclaimed.

"What?" Marty asked, looking at the page over her shoulder. "What erased?"

Jennifer frowned. Why was she staring at a blank piece of paper? And why had that paper been in her pocket?

"I don't know," she admitted. What importance could a blank piece of paper have, anyway? She was with Marty, now, and they were going to have a wonderful time together. That was what was really important, after all.

Marty pulled his truck to the side of the road, just before the railroad tracks. He had to come back here, one more time. He had been too upset when he'd left here earlier today to look through the wreckage of the DeLorean. But he had to, to find out if there was some way—any way—that he still might be able to rescue Doc.

"What are we doing here?" Jennifer called as Marty got out of the cab.

"I'll just be a minute," Marty called back. Actually, it might not even take that long. When that diesel had run over the DeLorean, it had done a pretty thorough job. Wreckage was scattered all along the tracks. Marty kicked a fender with his boot. Beyond it he saw a twisted piece of metal with the words MR. FUSION, and a bit torn from the time displays on the dashboard: LAST TIME DEPARTED.

But where was the flux capacitor? That was what really ran the time machine. If that particular mass of tubes and wires had somehow survived the crash, he might still be able to rescue Doc.

It took Marty a minute to realize he was looking right at it, a twisted bit of metal and glass beneath the time display. The glass cover had been shattered, and the inner workings were scrambled and bent. This flux capacitor would never work again.

There was a piece of paper stuck to the back of the twisted capacitor. Marty peeled it free and saw it was the photograph of Doc in front of the clock in 1885—or what was left of it. The photograph was burned through the middle, leaving Doc posing with only half a clock. Marty looked at it sadly. This was all that was left of Doc Brown.

Marty sighed as he looked one more time at the total wreckage around him. He hoped Doc was happy, wherever he was.

He looked up when he heard the sonic boom.

Jennifer jumped from the truck and ran to his side as they both stared at the steam locomotive rumbling down the tracks. It looked sort of like the locomotive Marty and Doc had stolen—or borrowed, as Doc put it—to get them back to the future. Except somebody had added a few things to the locomotive's working parts, coils, tubes, even a box with a Y shaped gizmo in it that looked a little like a flux capacitor. The whole engine looked like something out of Jules Verne as it braked to a stop beside them.

And Doc Brown waved at him from the cab.

"Marty!" the inventor called. "It runs on steam!"

Doc was wearing an engineer's cap and coveralls. And he wasn't alone. Behind him in the cab were Clara, a couple of small boys, and a dog that looked like Einstein.

"Oh, we tied the knot!" Doc exclaimed, waving at those behind him. "Meet the family! Clara you know, and these are my boys, Jules and Vern!" He smiled down at his sons. "Boys, this is Marty and Jennifer."

Doc got married? Doc had a family? Doc showed up here in a steam time machine? Marty didn't know what to say.

Clara waved. "Hi, Marty."

Marty guessed he'd better say something.

"Hi. Congratulations."

"Thank you," Clara replied with a smile.

Marty decided that now that he was getting over the shock, he was really glad to see his old friend again. He walked over to the locomotive.

"Doc. It's unbelievable. This is wonderful! And here I thought I'd never see you again!"

Doc grinned back at him. "You can't keep a good scientist down. After all, I had to come back for Einstein—and, well, I didn't want you to be worried about me."

He reached for something inside the cab. "Oh,

I brought you a little souvenir." He handed Marty a rectangular package, wrapped in brown paper with a red ribbon.

Marty tore the paper open. Inside was a framed photograph of Marty and Doc in front of the clock; the same photograph he'd found in the wreckage of the DeLorean, except now Marty was in the photograph!

He looked up at his friend. "I love it, Doc. Thanks."

"Then it wasn't a dream," Jennifer muttered at his side. He looked over to see her staring intently at a crumpled piece of paper that didn't seem to have anything on it. She looked up at the inventor.

"Doctor Brown, I just want to know one thing. What happens to Marty and me in the future?"

Doc considered her question for a second before answering. "In the future? That's up to you. Your future hasn't been written—no one's has. For better or worse, your future is what you make it." He winked at both Marty and Jennifer. "So make it a good one. Both of you."

Marty put his arm around Jennifer. "We will, Doc. And what about you? Are you going—back to the future?"

The inventor shook his head. "Nope. Already been there!"

He pushed a lever in the locomotive's cab, and with a rush of steam, the wheels folded underneath the engine and the entire locomotive lifted off the tracks. Doc and his family all waved as the locomotive rose twenty feet into the air and then proceeded to chug off into the afternoon sky.

After a moment, Marty and Jennifer remembered to wave back, until the locomotive was no more than a speck in the heavens.